Deditio Optio Non Est

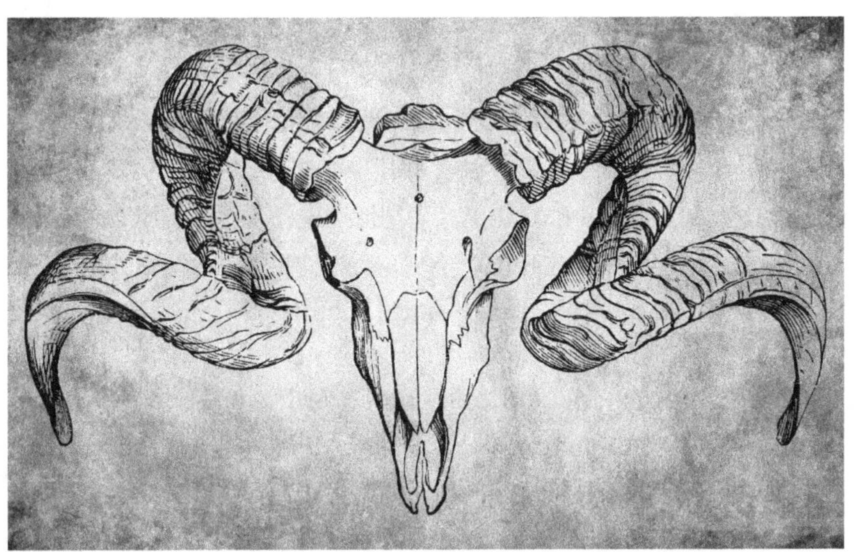

The Malum

Something dark and sinister came into our world. Those few who have seen it and lived know it only as the Malum in Latin. In English, it translates to, "The Evil." There are only a few of us who know exactly how it came to exist and how it made it through to our world. We know it had help getting here, and we know why it comes. It consumes people in droves as darkness settles in. As I write this, it's been several years since it all happened, but I'll try to remember how it started and provide as many details as possible. I was one of the few who saw it and lived to tell about it.

My name is James David Thieriot, but to my family and friends, I was JD. I was your average blond-haired, troubled teenager who loved hanging out with my friends, raising hell, playing hockey, and exploring the mountains behind my house. All of that changed on November 15th, 1985. It was my fifteenth birthday. It was also the day it entered our world again and the day my friends and I met it.

That day was supposed to be like any other birthday. My three best friends were over at my house to celebrate. Matt, the freckle-faced redhead who loved basketball; Jason, the suave, good-looking ladies' man; and Chung, who was always happy-go-lucky. He was a Chinese descendant but was born in Vietnam and raised in Maine. Being a Chinese descendant was important to him.

As is common with teenagers, my friends were like my brothers and were just as important to me as my own family. I mean, what teenager gets along with their family at that age, right? It's not until you get older that you realize family is everything, or for an unfortunate few, not until they're gone.

It was around 5:00 p.m., and we'd just eaten what would be my last slice of pizza from our local pizza shop, Main Street Pizza. Pizza was my favorite food, and Main Street Pizza was my favorite place to eat it. I also had the last slice of birthday cake I'd ever eat, but I had no way of knowing that at the time. After we finished eating, my friends and I decided we'd go for a short hike in the mountains behind my house. We had a few hours of sunlight left, which gave us plenty of time to explore. Being young and dumb, we didn't think about bringing a flashlight. After all, it was still light out when we set off exploring. My family had been living in the same house for about ten years at that point, and I'd explored most of the mountains in our neighborhood. There were only a couple of places I had never been in.

One such area was a really old cemetery. I'd never dared to go in, and there was a good reason for that. There was an old story that circulated in our town that the cemetery had belonged to a group of settlers who were thought to have been miners. It was said they'd been cast out and accused of using dark magic or witchcraft. Some folks said they were trying to get help from the dark side in their quest to find gold, while others said it was just out of pure evilness—no one really seemed to know for sure. Everyone in town knew the old stories, but what they let into this world was far worse than anything that resided in the dark corners of Hell.

My friend Matt had always pestered us to go check out this particular cemetery, but the rest of us never understood why I'd always refused. The four of us basically grew up in this area, on the same block, to be exact. So we all knew the old stories about the cemetery and had avoided it like the plague, until that day—a day I will never forget, as long as I'm aboveground.

On this particular day, though—I have a hard time remembering exactly why now, but I must've been weakminded, or maybe I was just tired of him asking—I reluctantly gave in. Our two other friends, Jason and Chung, were hesitant as well. I could tell they didn't want to go, but since

I had always been the leader of the group, they followed along once I said I would. So, we all took off for the cemetery. It was a several-mile hike into the particular grove of trees where the cemetery sits. We hadn't thought of the fact that it would be almost dark by the time we made it there, or that complete darkness would have set in on our hike back.

After we'd hiked for several miles, knowing we were getting very close to the cemetery, I heard a faint voice in the back of my head telling me to turn back and go home. However, I dismissed it as me being chicken shit. At fifteen, I wasn't about to let my friends think I was scared of some old bullshit stories. So onward we pressed, even though the voice in my head was screaming louder and louder with each step to turn back and go home.

As the cemetery came into view, a very dark, eerie feeling swept over me. It was almost like déjà vu, though much darker and different somehow. Again, I decided that I couldn't let my friends think I was a chicken or they'd never let me live it down, so I ignored the voice that was now screaming in my head, telling me to go home. As we slowly passed through the cemetery gates, it felt like we entered another world. All four of us instantly looked at each other, and we all knew we'd just experienced the same eerie feeling.

By now the sun was slowly creeping behind the mountains, and light was fading fast. As we were about to turn around and get the hell outta there, Matt looked back and noticed something in the middle of the cemetery, between a set of gravestones. It was a three-foot-high, shiny octagonal pillar. It was jet-black in color, and we could see the last bit of the sun's rays shining off of it. It was so shiny, in fact, it looked as if it'd been polished that very day. I immediately knew something was very wrong and was about to say, "Let's get outta here, guys," when Matt suddenly turned and walked straight over to it. I whispered loudly to him, "Matt, no! Let's go!" He didn't listen or hesitate a bit at the sound of my voice. He went straight to it, finally hesitated for only a split second, then reached out and touched it. The moment he touched the pillar, our lives changed forever.

It's hard to remember in detail exactly what happened next, but I do remember seeing a dark figure with long arms stretched out toward Matt. One thing I can vividly remember, though, were those hands, hands that had very long, black nails, reaching out for Matt. The next thing I faintly remember was me hitting the ground, and Matt letting out a blood-curdling scream that shook me to my very core. Then he was just *gone*. At that point, Jason and Chung were also letting out screams unlike anything I'd ever heard come out of them. They then pulled me up off the ground, and we took off running down the trail through the mountains as fast as our legs would carry us. We ran for what seemed like hours.

As we raced down that steep, pine-tree-covered mountain, our legs and faces hit what seemed like every tree branch and rock. As I was running, I kept hearing Matt's scream over and over again and was thinking, *We need to go back and get him.* I was in such a state of shock that what had happened hadn't fully registered with me yet. As we continued running through the darkness with only the moonlight to guide our way, Jason and Chung kept yelling, "Run! Run! Run!"

Looking back, I'm not quite sure how we even made it back home. I do remember stumbling into my parents' garage through the side door so they wouldn't know we'd come home. I was so completely exhausted, out of breath, and so full of adrenaline, I started throwing up pizza and birthday cake in the corner of the garage. I was also in excruciating pain from hitting so many rocks and branches during our mad flight home. We all looked like we'd just been in a fight, a fight where we had gotten our asses kicked. The three of us stood there looking at each other, trying to catch our breath.

Without it needing to be said aloud, the three of us knew we couldn't tell anyone about what had just happened. We knew no one would believe us.

The fact that we were all scratched and beat to hell would only make it worse and would make us suspects in our own friend's disappearance. We sat there all night in my parents' garage, looking at each other without uttering a word. The three of us were trying to figure out what the hell had just happened and where our best friend—our brother—Matt was. We knew something unfathomable had happened to him, but it just didn't make any sense or seem real. Deep down, though, we knew we would never see him again. We sat there in silence until the light of the sun came through the corner of the garage window.

Daylight was breaking, and we had no choice. We finally stood up and decided to move. We put our torn, blood-stained clothes into a garbage bag, then we each took a shower in the basement of my house, so we wouldn't wake my parents. After that we went outside and burned our clothes in the fire pit. We stood there in silence as we watched the fire consume our clothes. After the fire died down, we decided it was time to break the news to my parents that Matt had disappeared, but we knew we couldn't tell them the truth about what had happened to him.

We then went inside and woke my parents. Once we finished telling them our made-up version of what happened, my father picked up the phone and called the police. A search party was quickly organized, and within twenty minutes there were police cars, search and rescue trucks, and even fire engines parked out in front of my house, taking up the whole block. The police made it to my house first, of course, to question the three of us. They immediately separated us once they arrived, but unbeknownst to them, we had already made up a story and knew exactly what to say before we were even questioned. We knew our stories had to be exactly the same, which was that he'd simply walked off and disappeared into the darkness—nothing more. We knew we could never mention the black pillar or the dark figure, because if we did, they'd think we were not only crazy but guilty of foul play. Telling them the truth would solve nothing anyway. It would only create more trouble for us, and we knew it. There was nothing we could do to help Matt at this point anyway, so we figured the best thing we could do was try to protect each other.

After the police finished questioning us, Jason and Chung's parents came over to pick them up and asked us what had happened, but all we could say was what we'd told the police. He simply walked off into the darkness and disappeared. None of us ever mentioned the black pillar or the dark figure. Again, we knew they'd think we were crazy, and we'd instantly become suspects, if we weren't already. Matt's parents, Mac and Michelle, came over to my house not long after that. They were, of course, hysterical, asking where Matt was and what had happened, begging us to tell them where their son was. The only thing I could say, again, was that he had disappeared into the darkness.

That day was indeed a dark one for me.

LXVI

Once they finally left, I went upstairs to my bedroom and flopped down on my bed. I lay there staring at the ceiling for hours and hours, trying to piece together what had happened to my best friend, my brother, and what the hell the dark figure could have possibly been. To say I was terrified beyond comprehension would be an understatement.

I must've drifted asleep because I was suddenly awoken to the horrific sound of my mom screaming for me to come downstairs. It was dark outside when I awoke, so I knew it was at least past 9:00 p.m., which meant I'd been asleep for three or four hours. I immediately jumped off my bed and bolted down the stairs into the living room. My mom's face was white as a ghost, and she didn't utter a word. She just pointed to the TV. I turned and looked and could see the local news was on. I watched as they talked about the disappearance of my friend, Matthew Don

Mckell. The reporter then started talking, in an almost panicked state about how they'd lost contact with all of the search party teams that were up in the mountains searching for Matt. Which would've numbered in the several dozens. A chill went up my spine, and a sense of eeriness overcame me. I knew in that instant what had happened to them. The dark figure. At that point in time, I only knew to refer to it as the dark figure. It wouldn't be until later that I'd be able to put a name to it and would become all too familiar with it.

I sat in front of the TV for several hours, watching the hysteria unfold as the live news coverage filmed the authorities scrambling around in complete chaos, trying to get in contact with the police and rescuers who seemed to have vanished into thin air. The police sent several more small search parties and helicopters with huge spotlights up the mountain to try to find the missing parties, but they'd eventually end up losing contact with them as well.

I'm not exactly sure what time it was when I passed out from exhaustion, but I woke up to both of my parents standing in front of the TV. Their eyes were glued to the screen, and neither of them were saying a word. I will never forget the terrified looks on their faces.

My father eventually turned to look at me and said they'd lost contact with four separate search parties and two helicopters during the night. They planned on sending up another search party at first light.

He then walked over, sat down in front of me, and got less than six inches away from my face. He looked me square in the eyes and calmly asked me, "Son, what happened up there, exactly? Tell me the truth, not the bullshit you told the cops." I sat there for a few minutes contemplating what I should say while trying to figure out what was going on. I couldn't even process it all because it was happening too fast. It still seemed surreal, a nightmare that I was expecting to wake up from any minute.

At first, I stuttered to find the words while fighting back the tears, but I went into as much detail as I could remember. I didn't hold anything back. I laid it all down to the both of them. They sat there intently listening as I explained the black pillar, Matt going up and touching it, and the dark figure appearing. They didn't even flinch when I told them about the long, black nails, Matt letting out his blood-curdling scream, and then Matt disappearing. When I finished, though, they looked like someone had just ripped out their hearts. They could see the truth and horror in my face, and they knew I wasn't lying. They didn't say a word, just turned their attention back to the TV. I spent the rest of the day glued to the TV as well, waiting for an update, clinging to hope they'd all turn up, especially my best friend. Somewhere deep down, though, I knew I'd never see him again.

I didn't eat or drink at all that day and finally went to bed around midnight. The following morning, my mother came into my room and woke me up by handing me the phone. It was my friend Jason, and he started off by asking me if I'd told anyone the truth of what we'd seen. I didn't hesitate in telling him my parents now knew, and he said he had told his as well, and they believed him just like mine had. I said how could they not with everything that was going on with the police and search parties disappearing. We both agreed the police and search parties disappearing without a trace was definitely related to the dark figure that had taken Matt. When I asked him what his parents said when he told them, he said they didn't say a word. I told him that didn't surprise me because they were trying to process it as well, and they were surely just as scared as we are.

He asked me what we should do, and I said at the very least we needed to find out what had actually happened to Matt. We also needed to know what the hell the dark figure even was, and if there was anything that would stop it. I told him to call Chung and tell him to meet up for lunch at the One Man Band, which was a local 1950s diner we liked.

Around 12:30 p.m. the three of us showed up in front of the One Man Band. We stood there staring at each other for several minutes without saying a word. We didn't have to; we each knew what the other was thinking. We'd built such a strong bond over the years, it was as if we could read each other's minds.

We knew we had to find some answers. We owed it to our brother.

We went inside, sat down, and ordered some food. None of us were really hungry, though. There was only one thing on our minds. Chung started out asking the questions all of us were wondering. What the hell happened, and what the hell are we going to do about it? He was looking directly at me the whole time he was talking, so I knew he was looking to me for an answer. I wasn't sure what I should say at this point, since, of course, I didn't know any more than he did. The only thing that came to my mind was that we needed to find out if the stories about the cemetery were true. What we had seen was obviously not from this world, so we needed to look into the abnormal for answers. After we finished picking at our meals and eating very little, just enough to make the stomach pains go away, I suggested we go to the library to see if we could find any information. If there was any truth at all to the stories we'd all heard since we were kids, I figured that would be the place we could find them.

When we got to the library and walked inside, there was a decent-sized group of people huddled around the TV. Later in life, I realized that having a TV in a library was unusual, but our town's library had always had one, for as long as I could remember. Anyway, we knew exactly what they would all be watching and didn't even bother looking up at the TV. We pushed our way through the crowd, focused on accomplishing what we came to do. We did hear the news lady say four large groups of policemen, rescuers, and two helicopters had yet to be found. We also noticed people were starting to panic. We looked at each other and knew this wasn't going to stop. Something horrible and evil was happening right in our own town. We walked up to the librarian working the front desk and told her what we were looking for, and she pointed us in the right direction. We found three fairly thick books that were each written by different authors regarding our town's history. We each grabbed one, sat down, and started to read.

I started skimming through the book I'd grabbed until I came to the time period that talked about the settlers and the cemetery. I'd never known that the name of the cemetery where Matt disappeared was Smith's Cemetery. It was named after the settlers who buried the first person there, essentially creating the cemetery, and most of the settlers were related anyway, sharing the last name Smith. There was, however, another family named Verwer living in the area at the same time. The book said the name Verwer was Dutch, and the Verwers had immigrated to America from the Netherlands in 1880, with the sole purpose of meeting up with one of the Smith families. It said both families had originally met up in New Hampshire once they'd gotten to America, and it wasn't long after that they started to get persecuted for their beliefs in the occult, to the point of being threatened with death. They were eventually run out of New Hampshire, so they migrated to the hills of Maine, to a place where they could practice their dark beliefs in secrecy. This happened to be the very city where I lived and had since birth.

There weren't a lot of details regarding what happened to them after they moved to Maine. It did say that all of them suddenly disappeared one day, except for two young girls from the Verwer family. The girls ended up leaving Maine, and it was rumored they moved out west to the desert, somewhere in Utah. There was a photo of the cemetery and the two young girls. As I was looking at the photo, I was overcome with horror. Directly behind the two young girls stood the same shiny black pillar Matt had touched. I immediately showed my friends the photograph and explained what I'd just read. They had the same look of horror on their faces as their eyes locked on the pillar, seeming so prominent in the picture of the cemetery, since we knew how dangerous it was. I asked them if they'd found out anything. Jason said he found some journal entries from the closest neighbor to the Verwers and Smiths, which was about a quarter of a mile away. The entry said both families kept mostly to themselves, only venturing into town when they absolutely needed to, which was usually for supplies. That last journal entry talked about their disappearance and how it took place on November 15th, 1888. Hearing that sent chills up my spine. The 15th was my birthday, the date this all started.

The journal entry read as told by the neighbor who reported the incident to the authorities:

"Last night, right before dusk, as I was putting my horse Tilly into the barn having just returned home from town, I heard a loud shriek in the distance. The shriek was so horrible it stopped me dead in my tracks. I stood there for several long minutes without moving, only clutching Tilly's bridle in my hand. Then I started to hear shriek after shriek. This went on for several more minutes, then everything abruptly stopped. There was nothing but eerie silence. It was so silent, in fact, I could hear my own heart trying to jump out of my chest. I immediately ran into the house to tell Rebecca what I'd just heard. She said she'd heard it as well, and it made her drop the apple pie that she had been holding. I could see it in a mess on the floor. We both knew better than to venture up there—everyone knew something wasn't quite right with those two families. We decided it was best to stay inside with the doors locked and shotgun in hand. We'd go into town tomorrow to let Sheriff Brady know what we'd heard.

"The following morning we went into town and told Sheriff Brady what we'd heard. He quickly rounded up several deputies, a few other local men, and we rode up to the Smith and Verwer cabins. When the two cabins came into sight, we stopped the horses about fifty yards away, wanting to get a good look around before getting any closer. As we looked around, we could see that nothing appeared out of the ordinary, other than the fact that the doors to both cabins were wide open. We proceeded to shout for them to come out, but we got no reply. We got off our horses and, with guns drawn, walked ever so slowly toward the cabins. The first cabin we went into was dark and had a horrible smell to it. It smelled like a rotting animal carcass. We checked all of the bedrooms and closets and found nothing. We then went into the second cabin, which was about twenty yards away, and it smelled worse than the first one.

"After we'd checked the first two rooms upstairs in the second cabin, we heard a faint noise coming from the closet in one of the back bedrooms. We walked very slowly through the bedroom with guns raised as we opened the closet door. What we found left us dumbfounded. Inside were two small girls who looked almost like identical twins. One had to be eight years of age, and the other looked to be around six or seven. They were very dirty and were covered from head to toe in blood. Not one inch of their little bodies was without blood. They were shaking uncontrollably, and their eyes were rolled back into their heads. Sheriff Brady knelt in front of the girls and asked them what happened and where their families were. They just stood there with horrified looks on their faces, not saying a word. He asked them several more times, but they didn't respond. They were, however, mumbling something ever so faintly, over and over again, in what seemed to be another language. That was the scariest moment of my life. I left that cabin that day a different man than I went in, and I was never the same.

"We then gathered up the girls and took them into town, where they lived with a local family for several months. The rumor is, a relative showed up one day out of nowhere and took them to southern Utah. Before they left town, they were questioned repeatedly by several different people, but they never uttered a word to anyone. It was said, though, they could be heard late at night, whispering to one another in strange tongues."

LXVI

As the three of us sat there, trying to piece together what we'd just read, a loud, booming voice in a deep, thick British accent said from directly behind me, "Boys! Are you the three who were at the Smith Cemetery when the boy disappeared?" I immediately turned around to look at who'd just scared the piss outta me and realized I was looking at kneecaps. I slowly lifted my gaze up toward his face and could see he was a very tall man with silver hair that looked almost like silk hanging down to his shoulders. His face looked like stone. *Damn! This man must be almost seven feet tall!* I thought.

The next thing he said as he lowered his voice to a loud whisper was, "I'm Crowley. I know what happened to your friend. We're all in serious danger if we don't stop it."

I stumbled to find a response, so for a few seconds, I just sat there with a stupid look on my face. I'm not sure if it was because of his size, his booming voice, or because of what he'd just said. I finally did manage to spit some words out. "Yes . . . that's us, and it was our friend Matt who disappeared."

"If we don't figure out how to stop this thing, we're all going to disappear," he responded.

"Well, how do you know that, and exactly how did you find us?" I asked.

"That's not important right now, but you'll find out in time. I see you boys are doing some studying."

He then asked us to tell him exactly what happened that night. So we laid it all down, just like we'd done with our parents, leaving no details out. As we went into gruesome detail about the dark figure and Matt, he didn't flinch a bit. He didn't seem surprised or taken aback by anything we said. He sat there intently listening to every bit of it. After we finished, the three of us sat in silence, waiting for him to respond. A few minutes went by before he said anything, then he calmly stated, "People will keep disappearing, and it will continue to spread as it gets stronger. People have no idea what they're dealing with."

Right then I jumped in and asked, "Yeah, so, if you know so much, exactly what in the hell *are* we dealing with?"

"All I can tell you right now is that there are two types of evil that exist. The type of evil we as men know of, such as serial killers and terrorists. Then there's what we call *dark evil*. Dark evil is what took your friend. Dark evil is so horrific you'd wish you were dead before it sinks its claws into you. What you'll experience once it gets a hold of you is far worse than any death a human on Earth has ever been dealt. I can't say exactly what it is, but I do know it's not from this world. It's an evil unlike anything the modern world has ever known, and it's been released into our world once again. It will keep consuming people until it's stopped. Now, we're not one hundred percent certain, but from what little we do know, there's a possibility it's been here before and has consumed millions of people, possibly whole civilizations. Ever heard of the Mayans? If it has been here once before, that means it's been stopped and must be stopped once again."

"Well, why tell us this? What the hell can we possibly do?" I asked.

"We need to track down any remaining Verwer family members to see if they have any new information on what we're dealing with," replied Crowley.

"New information?" I asked. He just looked at me with a straight face and didn't answer. "Well, good luck with that, because that family could be anywhere," I said.

"You now know, and I know, the two surviving Verwer girls' last known location was supposedly in the desert of southern Utah. That's where we'll start. Go home now and get some rest. We're leaving when the sun rises. You three meet me at the One Man Band diner tomorrow morning at sunrise, and don't be late."

Crowley then turned around and walked out of the library. The three of us just looked at each other, shaking our heads in disbelief at what we'd just heard. We knew what Crowley had told us was the truth. We also knew we had to go with him if we wanted the answers we were seeking.

LXVI

When I arrived home it was already dark, and my parents were still in front of the TV. They looked like someone had just sucked the life right out of them. They asked me where I'd been, and I said that I'd been at the library with my friends. I'd made the decision before I got home that I wasn't going to tell them about our plans with Crowley the next day. They would, of course, try to stop me, and I knew that it was something I had to do.

They barely seemed to process what I was saying to them anyway, and when I asked them what was wrong, they told me about something that had happened just minutes before I got home. They had been watching the news reporter talk about what had been happening locally, when there was a quick flash of black followed by horrible screaming. The camera suddenly dropped, hitting the ground with a thud, then nothing—they were just gone. The news then cut to the reporters back at the station, and they stated they weren't sure what happened but that they would update everyone as soon as they were able to find out more information.

As I sat down with my parents and started watching the news, they kept replaying that moment over and over again. As I watched the flash appear and reappear, I knew it was the dark figure. I knew my parents knew that as well, but they were too afraid to say it. This was something far outside of anyone's realm of reality. For me, it was becoming more and more of a reality, and an ever-deepening sense of despair.

After watching the slow-mo replay several times, I quietly made my way to my bedroom and shut the door. I didn't feel like eating or talking to anyone, even though I hadn't eaten much of anything over the last twenty-four hours. I just needed to absorb everything that was happening around me. My head was spinning like an out-of-control carousel. I started thinking mostly about Crowley and how we were planning to leave Maine and head to Utah the next day. I thought, *I have school tomorrow, and what the hell do I say to my parents? Should I make up a lie? Do I just disappear?* I made the decision it was best to just leave a note rather than argue with them about it. After sitting on my bed for a while, I finally stood up and started to pack some things I was going to take with me.

It wasn't long after that, I zonked out into a deep sleep. After what seemed like only minutes, I was awoken to the sound of my alarm screaming in my ear. I reached over and slammed the off button. I knew in that moment, my life would never be the same. I threw the covers off, stood up, changed my clothes, grabbed my pack, and slowly and quietly opened my bedroom door. I looked into the hallway to see if the coast was clear, and it was. As quietly as I could, I crept past my parents' bedroom, thankful the door was shut. Part of me wanted to see them one last time before I left, but I knew how headstrong they were. They would definitely not be cool with their only child leaving the state on a road trip with a stranger. Someone I'd literally just met the day before.

I made my way downstairs and put the note I had written for them on the kitchen counter. I took one last look around, not knowing if I'd ever be back, before I took off out the back door. As I was walking down the sidewalk in front of my house, I could see Jason and Chung also coming out of their houses, as we all lived on the same block. As I stood there waiting for them, I paused and looked back at my house and wondered what was in store for us next. I knew I owed it to my friend, my brother, Matt, to try to find out what had actually happened to him. We also had to try to stop the dark figure, and the only way to do that might be out west with Crowley.

We'd agreed to meet at the One Man Band diner so we could grab some breakfast before hitting the road. The three of us all happened to show up a few minutes earlier than Crowley. He then seemed to come out of nowhere, popping up right behind us, scaring the shit out of us again with his loud, booming voice.

"Morning, boys! Are you ready?"

"As ready as I can be, I guess, given what's been going on around us the last few days," I replied.

"I understand, but it grows worse each day. No matter what the costs are, we must stop it before it consumes all of us," said Crowley.

"Yeah, I know. I watched the news last night," I replied.

I wasn't sure if he meant consuming just us or all of humanity. I guess I didn't really want to know. One thought did come to my mind, though: if we didn't stop it, who would?

We went inside to eat breakfast before hitting the road. After eating Hank's Country Breakfast, my favorite meal from the One Man Band, we made our way outside and climbed into Crowley's black 1977 Chevelle. He fired up the engine, and we sped off down the highway that would take us due west and out of Bangor. As we sped along on the highway, I noticed Crowley had a strange-looking black arrowhead hanging from his rearview mirror. It was about the size of a shot glass and appeared to be rather old.

None of us said much those first few hours. I imagine my friends, like me, were replaying the events that had unfolded over the last couple of days in their minds. I know I sure was. As we drove, Crowley had a cassette of Lynyrd Skynyrd cranked up in the car. When the song "Free Bird" came on I couldn't help but think of Matt and all the good times we had together as we were growing up. My mind then turned to his blood-curdling screams, and that replayed in my mind over and over again. Tears started rolling down my cheeks as I thought of the pain he must've felt when the dark figure got a hold of him. He was one of my best friends, my brother, my family. Thinking I would never see him again was almost too much to bear.

We must've driven at least eight hours before Crowley suggested we stop, get something to eat, and settle in for the night. We pulled off the freeway and found a local greasy spoon to grab a bite. We all ordered burgers and fries. After wolfing down dinner and making some small talk, we walked over to the motel that was next door. Crowley said it'd be best to share a room and not be separated. I agreed, and I imagine Chung and Jason felt safer being with Crowley as well.

As we entered the room, I immediately walked over to turn on the TV because I wanted to see if there was any news from back home. I was about to hit the power button on the remote when Crowley said in his usual booming voice, "No, boy, do not turn it on! We don't need the distraction right now, and there's no turning back. We need to press forward no matter what's happening back home."

I understood what he was saying and knew it wouldn't do any good to watch it anyway.

Our room only had two king beds, so we decided Crowley would have his own bed, Jason and Chung would share one, and I'd take the small sofa in the corner. Not that I'd get much sleep no matter where I ended up.

As we were getting ready to settle in, Crowley suddenly started pushing the sofa I was going to sleep on over by the two king beds. I watched intently as he then moved both beds about a foot away from the wall. He reached into his battered green army duffle bag and pulled out an old brown leather bag. He opened it up and began pouring black sand onto the floor, making a full circle that completely surrounded the beds and sofa. After pouring out all of the sand, he pulled out what looked to be an old painting of a ram's skull. The painting was black as well. He set the painting in the middle of the circle, then knelt down, closed his eyes, and began chanting something that none of us could quite hear. The three of us looked at each other and shrugged our shoulders. It looked almost like he was praying. After Crowley stood up, he looked at us and said, "Under no circumstances, no matter what happens, are you to leave this circle after you go to sleep. You gotta piss, you hold it in. Got it?"

We all just nodded our heads in agreement. None of us dared question him or ask what the hell the black sand and ram's skull was for. Crowley was still very intimidating to us at that point.

I went and laid down on the sofa. I must've dozed off in seconds because that next thing I remember was being jolted awake by Jason, who was shaking me, saying, "Come on, man, we're leaving."

I looked out the window and could see it was still dark. I could also see Crowley was already in his Chevelle, warming up the engine. I turned around to grab my stuff and leave and noticed the black sand and the skull painting were gone, not a trace of it left.

When I opened the car door to get in, Crowley looked at me and said in a serious tone, "Get in, boy, we must hurry. It grows worse each day."

I knew what he meant, and he didn't have to tell me twice. He backed the Chevelle up and sped off down the road. As we were driving along, Crowley told us about how bad things were getting back home. He didn't go into much detail other than a lot of people were disappearing, and it was spreading farther out each night. He compared it to a forest fire, to help us understand the damage. Right then, I thought of my parents and hoped they were smart enough to get the hell outta town before it got to them, which I was assuming they had. My dad was always fairly smart and, for the most part, exercised common sense when he made decisions, so I wasn't too worried. As I was thinking about them, we passed a sign that said we'd just entered Ohio, so we were well on our way. We still had a day or two, though, depending on how fast we drove.

It didn't take long before I drifted off to sleep. Next thing I knew, I was jolting awake. I realized I was sitting in the car all alone, and it was dark outside. This was surprising to me. I must've really been tired because I was usually a very light sleeper. In the past, I would've woken up for sure when Crowley and my friends opened the car's doors, but for some reason, I hadn't this time. I was out like a light.

As I was sitting there in the car, I suddenly got the strangest feeling that something was behind me. I could feel something breathing on my neck, and there was a horrible smell that seemed to surround me. Something then whispered in my ear in the most god-awful voice I'd ever heard, "I'm coming, James."

My mind was screaming at me to turn around and look, but my body was frozen stiff. I looked down and saw a set of black fingers with long, sharp black nails slowly moving across my chest toward my heart. The claws then plunged into my chest, and I experienced the worst pain I've ever felt. It was like a dump truck had just slammed into me. I let out a hideous scream and started to shake uncontrollably. As I was shaking, more and more violently, the god-awful voice kept repeating my name over and over: "James, James, James."

I almost jumped out of my seat and was startled out of my dream. I noticed my clothes were soaking wet with sweat, and Chung was shaking my shoulder, trying to wake me up.

"Dude, what the hell happened?" asked Chung.

"Holy shit! I just had the most horrific nightmare of my life," I replied as I was trying to catch my breath. I was telling them what had happened in my dream when Crowley looked at me and cut me off mid-sentence.

"Was the dark figure in it?" asked Crowley.

"It was. How did you know?" I asked.

"I've been having the same nightmare as well, since the day it was released," said Crowley.

We drove for a few more hours before deciding we were starving. We agreed to stop for something to eat. We pulled off the main highway and found a little waffle diner that sounded good. When we got out of the car and walked into the diner, we immediately noticed a crowd of people standing in front of the TV, talking amongst themselves. We couldn't hear what any of them were saying to each other, but we could see they were in a state of panic. We all looked at each other and knew what they were panicking about. We moved closer so we could hear exactly what the reporters on TV were saying. The headline across the screen read:

"Hundreds, if not thousands, have disappeared from Bangor, Maine, and surrounding towns."

The reporter went on to say that people had been disappearing in droves as darkness set in each night, and it seemed to be spreading farther out each time. They had a map displayed that had the exact spots marked where people had last been seen. The starting point, of course, was Smith Cemetery.

The reporter said the National Guard had been called in as well as the FBI and that they had been doing their searching during the daylight hours and leaving the affected areas before dark. I thought, *Well, at least they're getting smarter about it.* I knew they still had no idea what they were dealing with. I mean, how could they? I had actually seen it, and I still had no idea what the thing was. After several more minutes, our stomachs reminded us that we were starving and we had to eat, regardless of what was happening.

We went and sat down at a booth and waited for the waitress to come take our order. After we ordered our food, I asked, "Where are we, Crowley? What state are we in?"

"We're in the middle of Kansas," he replied.

"I'm curious to know exactly what our plan is when we get to Utah?" I asked.

Crowley responded, "It's rumored that the remaining Verwer family members moved to a small coal-mining town in Utah by the name of Orangeville. We're going there first, to see if we can find them, or at least turn something up. If we do happen to find them, we need to determine whether they know anything that could be useful in our current situation. It's highly likely they have new information, like I mentioned before."

"How do you know the name of the town?" I asked. He didn't say anything, just looked at me with a slight grin. He certainly was hiding something, that much was obvious, but I couldn't figure out why. Our food came out then, and all I could think about was making the rumbling in my stomach go away. I decided not to push him any further, but there were definitely some unexplained things about Crowley that made me nervous.

After we finished devouring our food, we stood up to leave. On our way out, we noticed that the crowd of people were still huddled around the TV, and we could see the fear in their eyes. People knew something very bad was happening. Fear of the unknown is often the worst experience.

We proceeded walking out of the restaurant and climbed into the Chevelle. Crowley fired up the engine, and once again, we hit the pavement.

This time we drove all through the night, and as we drove through the darkness, it seemed as if there weren't many cars on the road. It was just dead. Anytime we'd stop on the side of the road for a quick bathroom break, there was an eerie, uncomfortable silence outside.

LXVI

When the sun's first rays hit us the following morning we were in Colorado, and we could see the Rocky Mountains all around us. To me, it was quite a sight seeing the Rockies up close, having grown up in Maine and having spent my whole life within its borders. Mid-November found the leaves having fallen off the trees, leaving the mountains somewhat bare. It was still a sight to behold, though.

My perspective on life had completely changed over the last couple of days. I looked at things more closely and with more heart, rather than flying by the seat of my pants all the time. Thinking back, I realized, up until that fateful moment, I was only interested in hockey, getting girls, and hanging out with my buddies. And now that one of my brothers was missing and most likely dead, the thought of that brought despair, which shifted things into a different perspective. I realized how many things I'd taken for granted up to that point. I had a very difficult time grasping the concept that my life would be forever changed—things could never be the same.

We drove for what seemed like an eternity before we hit the desert and, finally, the Utah border. As we crossed the border into Utah, a dark sense of eeriness came over me. I could sense we were getting closer to the answers we were looking for, and I knew we might not like what we were going to find.

Suddenly, out of the blue, Crowley looked over at me and said, "Boy, pull the map out of the glove compartment. I'll need directions to Orangeville from here."

As I pulled out the map and looked at it, I could see we were only a hundred miles or so from Orangeville, so we decided to drive on through without stopping. I gave Crowley directions and then dozed off again. The next thing I remember was Crowley grabbing me by the arm and telling me we had arrived. It was dark at the time, but from what I could see, it looked like we were on the town's main street. Orangeville's main street, to be exact. It looked like something out of the 1950s, almost like time had skipped over it and kept right on going. Crowley said it was about 11:45 p.m., so obviously too late to try to find the Verwer farm, if they were even here at all. We decided to find a motel to stay the night. It just so happened there was only one motel in the entire town, so that made it easy. The furniture and TV inside looked old, as old as the town itself.

Just like before, Crowley laid the black sand down, making a full circle, then put the painting of the ram's skull in the middle, then chanted something. At this point, we were all pretty much hammered from having traveled such a long distance in a short period of time, and we all immediately crashed, except for Crowley, that is.

When I woke up, the sun was hitting my face. I looked over and saw Crowley sitting in the exact same chair he had been in when I'd fallen asleep.

"Crowley, have you been sitting there awake the whole night?" I asked.

He replied, "Yes, we can't afford to let our guard down now that we're most likely getting closer to the Verwer family."

I wasn't sure how he could survive on such little sleep, but it didn't seem to affect him one bit.

Crowley said, "Get up, boys. Let's get ready and get something to eat." Jason and Chung both groaned but rolled off the bed. We got ready and found a local diner to grab a bite to eat.

As we walked into the diner, it was easy to see this town didn't get many outsiders because everyone was staring at us like we were fresh-out-of-prison convicted felons. The waitress was quite nice, though, so as she was taking our order, we asked her if she knew who the Verwers were and if they lived around here.

At first she gave us a long, blank stare and then asked, "Whatcha all want with them?"

Crowley spoke before we could. "Oh, we're just distant relatives looking to connect with them again."

She looked at Crowley for a minute, then said, "I think the Verwers still have a farm up on the old dirt road, on Vineyard Lane. No one sees them much. They like to keep to themselves."

"Well, ma'am, how do we find the old dirt road?" Crowley asked.

At that point, everyone in the diner immediately turned around to look at us. They all had blank, uncomfortable stares on their faces. It was as if Crowley had just called her an obscene name or something.

She leaned in closer to us and replied in a loud whisper, "You'll want to drive south out of town until you see the sign for Vineyard Lane. Turn left at the sign and go up that road until you hit the old dirt road. You'll drive down that road for several miles, until you come to the Verwer farm on the left."

I made a mental note the Verwer family lived somewhat far away from town, like their ancestors in Maine had done. This made me uneasy.

After eating a quiet and uncomfortable breakfast, we left the diner and took off for the Verwer farm.

As we were driving, I could tell my friends were feeling just as uneasy as I was, which seemed like a normal reaction to me. What didn't feel normal was Crowley. He seemed perfectly content and postured, like he knew what was going to happen and this was all part of the plan.

When we hit the old dirt road, I could see weeds growing down the middle, weeds that were at least three feet high. That meant no one had driven down the road in a long time. As we continued forward, there were fields of wheat and corn as far as the eye could see, rolling hills of it.

When the Verwer farm finally came into sight, Jason, Chung, and I all looked at each other with worried faces.

Crowley proceeded to drive slowly past the house, and I noticed that he made it a point to turn the front of the car toward the dirt road as he parked. I assumed it was in case we had to leave in a big damn hurry.

The sun was getting higher in the sky now, and it had to be mid-morning. As Crowley parked the car and slowly turned off the engine, we could all see the house and barn were very old and run-down. There were two old rusted vehicles parked in front of the house, an old station wagon and an old Ford pickup.

Crowley looked at the three of us and said in a stern, almost intimidating, voice, "Under no circumstances are you boys to step foot outside of this car, no matter what happens. Understood?" We nodded our heads in agreement, none of us much interested in leaving the relative safety of the car anyway. "I'm leaving the keys in the ignition in case something happens to me. If something does happen, you get the hell outta here as fast as you can."

Right as Crowley stepped out of the Chevelle, we all noticed someone looking out through the kitchen window, and we could almost feel the heat of them glaring at us. The front door slowly creaked open, and out came a man who looked like he was straight out of the movie *Deliverance*. He even had a long stem of wheat hanging out of his mouth. He looked at Crowley, then calmly moved his glare over at us and said, "Whatcha all want? I don't know who the hell you people are."

In that moment, I noticed the black arrowhead Crowley had hanging from his rearview mirror was changing color, from black to white.

Crowley then turned his head back around, looking directly at the arrowhead as well. He slowly and calmly started moving his hands behind his back and up his jacket, like he was reaching for something. He then asked the man, "Are you the third generation of Verwers?"

The man just stood there for a minute, looking at us while twirling the stem of wheat in his mouth, not saying a word. After what seemed like several minutes, he finally spoke up and said, "You're all here about what's happening out east, aren't ya? I know what you are. I sensed you as soon as you hit the dirt road."

My heart immediately sank, and I thought, *Oh shit, we're in trouble.* Little did I know at the time exactly what the man was and what he was capable of doing.

The man then said with a slight grin, "It's getting worse, ya know. Soon it'll be outside of Maine." He then paused for a moment and said with the evilest of grins, "You're all gonna die. You can't stop the darkness that's comin'. You can't stop the Malum."

As he finished his last sentence, a noise caught our attention, and we all turned to look back to our right. We could hear the barn door start loudly creaking as it slowly opened. Right then, we noticed a set of long, black nails just like the ones the three of us had seen when Matt was killed. It was pushing the door open from the inside. But it suddenly stopped and quickly went back inside once sunlight hit it.

Without muttering another word, the man Crowley had been talking to took off on a dead run back into the house, dropping the stem of wheat from his mouth as he ran. What happened next is hard to remember in vivid detail, but I do remember Crowley jumping into the car, firing up the Chevelle's V8 engine, and laying a patch of gravel and dirt as he sped off down the old dirt road.

Before I could even ask him what the hell was going on, Crowley said, "That family is part of what's happening. I just needed confirmation is all.

I'd bet my life if we were to go into that barn, we'd find another black pillar, much like the one you saw in the old cemetery," said Crowley.

Now it was starting to make a little more sense to me, and I suddenly blurted out in my haste, "Well, what the fuck are we going to do, Crowley?"

Crowley looked directly at me and replied, "I thought this might happen. His ancestors were cast out for delving into the dark arts, as you know, but I was hoping it would've died with them at the cabin. This is turning out to be much worse than I expected."

As we sped along the dirt road and out onto the highway heading south, none of us said a word. I noticed as we hit asphalt that Jason and Chung hadn't uttered a single word since the farm. This started to worry me because I knew where I was at mentally, and it was not a good place to be. I turned and looked back at them and asked them if they were okay, but they didn't respond. They just stared out the car's windows into the distance. At that point I let things be and decided it was best if I kept my mouth shut. What could I really say anyway? It's not like I could reassure them that everything was going to be okay.

It was a while before anyone spoke again, and it was actually Jason who broke the silence. "We need to come up with a damn good plan if we decide to go back there again. The dark figure, the Malum, whatever the hell it is, will certainly kill us."

Crowley looked back at Jason through the rearview mirror, then turned his gaze back to the road and replied, "Most certainly we will die if we go back unprepared. It knows who you all are, and it now knows who I am."

"Yeah, who the hell are you anyways? You seem to know a lot more than you've been letting on," I asked, fed up with being kept in the dark.

He then uttered a name I knew well because I'd been a big fan of Ozzy Osbourne, ever since I was ten years old. I had always liked the song "Mr. Crowley." The name he uttered was, "Aleister Crowley." It didn't take me long to put two and two together, knowing he was Crowley as well. I'd assumed from the beginning that was his last name anyways.

LXVI

He told us his father was Aleister Crowley. He said his father was always misunderstood by the masses. He said that his father being famously accused of being an occultist, a devil worshiper, and an outright evil man was a flat-out lie, or he was simply misunderstood. In fact, the truth was quite the opposite. His father had been fighting "dark evil" as Crowley called it, ever since his father was a young man. He had spent most of his life trying to keep dark evil from entering the world and wiping out mankind.

He then proceeded to tell us a story I will never forget, no matter how many years I remain on this planet.

Aleister Crowley was, of course, born in England, as most people knew, back in 1875, joining a fairly wealthy family. They were very successful brewers, and this allowed Aleister the time and freedom to do what he wanted, which mostly included studying various things of interest. He happened to turn a lot of his attention toward the occult and dark magic. He inevitably became a leading expert on the subject, hence the reason he was always accused of being evil and practicing the occult, though the opposite was actually true. Aleister wanted to use what he'd learned to protect our world and to stop evil from entering it.

During his research, Aleister discovered something so sinister and evil that it shook him to his very core. To those few who knew of its existence, it was known as "dark evil."

Aleister was twenty-five years old the night he first came into contact with dark evil. He said it was a type of evil that modern man had never experienced, and it had the capability to wipe mankind from Earth if it was ever unleashed.

Crowley told us about the day his father, Aleister, first came in contact with dark evil. It was October 31st, Halloween, back in the year 1900.

Aleister was sitting in his study by candlelight writing down detailed notes on something new he'd just learned that very day. He'd discovered there were certain types of dark witches in Europe who were trying to use their dark magic to open our world to a darker realm they called, "Tenebris." The translation was "darkness."

How he came across this information was even more mysterious and eerie than what he was learning. Someone had left an old journal on his doorstep, completely anonymously. There was a note attached to it with his name on it. The note also said it had belonged to a dark witch who lived several hundred years ago in Norway.

The majority of the journal was written in Norwegian. There were some parts of the journal that had side notes written in English that talked about how the dark witches were trying to create a doorway that would allow "dark evil" to enter the world. As Aleister was writing down his own notes from what he was learning, he suddenly heard something whisper in his ear, right behind him, "Aleister." It sounded almost like hissing, and Aleister immediately stood up and froze.

It hissed his name again, but this time it said something else: "Aleister, join us or suffer." He immediately jumped away from his desk and turned around. What he saw was something so horrific it shook every cell in his body, and he was never the same man after that day.

Aleister stood there, frozen, unable to move for quite some time. Once he was able to move his legs again, he quickly sat down and started writing down every detail of what had just taken place, including his feelings about the event. The closest emotion he could describe as he wrote was "utter dread" and "absolute fear." He said the one detail he shall never forget about the dark being was its long, black nails. He wrote about how they were reaching out for him and how he was unable to move a muscle, having been totally paralyzed with fear.

On that night, Aleister vowed to stop dark evil from ever being allowed to enter our world. He knew if the dark realm was unleashed it could be the end of mankind. Aleister also knew he had to trace the origin of the book, and the only way to do that was to go to Norway.

Being a single man at the time, and not having to go to a day-to-day job due to his family's vast wealth, he didn't waste any time before setting off for Norway. The journal had entries of certain cities in Norway that were fairly close together geographically, so that's where he planned to start. Norway being fairly close to England as well, he figured it wouldn't be more than a few days' trek by boat and then carriage. It would actually take longer by carriage than by boat once he reached the mainland of Norway being his destination was Hammerfest, a small town in the northern region.

It was early November when Aleister set out on his trek. Crowley said his father described Norway as being, "colder than hell itself." He also said it

was very barren, nothing but treeless mountains and rolling hills. He said
he would go days without seeing another living soul other than the
carriage driver and his translator, a gentleman he'd hired in Oslo to
accompany him to Hammerfest. Along the way, he got to know his
translator quite well. Eventually, they discussed his purpose for going to
Hammerfest. Aleister being who he was didn't hold anything back but
told him everything in great detail. He said after that, the translator never
smiled or laughed again. He sat mostly in silence for the rest of the trip.

Once they arrived in Hammerfest, the translator said it would be best to
check out the local pubs to start asking questions. He told Aleister not to
expect people to warm up to them and warned him of the possibility of
negative confrontations with the locals.

Speaking of dark things such as witchcraft or dark magic is taboo in
Northern Norway. He told Aleister of the Vardo Witch Trials, which took
place in the very town they were in, back in 1621. He said the locals still
believed in it, and it still very much affected their daily lives.

The translator said it was the first major witch trial of Northern Norway,
and one of the biggest witch trials ever in Scandinavia. The Vardo Witch
Trials took place in the spring of 1621. A woman by the name of Mari
Jorgensdatter was accused of being a witch. When the locals captured
her, she was severely beaten and tortured for days on end before finally
confessing to being a dark witch. She confessed that on Christmas night
in 1620, she was suddenly awoken to a dark being standing at the edge of
her bed. The dark being said it was from another realm, and it asked her
to accept and worship dark evil in exchange for eternal life. She accepted.

She said the dark being then gave her a "witch's brand" by biting her
hand between her fingers on her left hand. She was then instructed to
recruit other women who were willing to accept it as she did. Mari
brought ten more women to the dark being before finally being caught by
her fellow townsfolk. It was rumored that when she was caught, she was

so severely beaten and tortured that she was struggling just to breathe when she confessed. She was then dragged by horses out into the middle of town, tied to a cross, and burned alive. The townsfolk who watched her burn said she let out the most horrific screams and cursed them as the skin melted off her bones.

On April 28th, 1621, the rest of the ten women were sentenced to death as well. Instead of being tied to crosses and burned, they were thrown down into the bottom of an empty well and buckets of oil were poured on them. A torch was then lit and thrown down into the well. They screamed in horror as they were burned alive for sorcery. The townsfolk said the smell of the burning bodies lingered in town for several months, even though the well was several miles away from town. The well was then covered and sealed forever, but not before throwing what was left of Mari Jorgensdatter's body into the well with the ten others. The events of that year had haunted the town ever since.

The first local pub Aleister and the translator went into was called the Kaikanten. As they walked in, there were half a dozen men sitting around a table, talking and laughing as a barmaid worked behind the counter. As they walked farther into the bar the men at the table suddenly ceased talking and laughing and turned to look at Aleister and the translator. The translator quietly said, "I'm going to introduce us and tell them why we're here, so be prepared for any kind of reaction."

As the translator began to speak, Aleister's attention was drawn to something on the wall. It was a strange-looking symbol, almost exactly like a symbol he'd seen in the witch's journal. The symbol looked as if two crescent moons were facing each other with an eight-sided black star in the middle of the moons. Seeing this put Aleister on alert and immediately made him suspicious. He turned his attention back to the translator, who was still talking. Aleister could see that everyone was looking directly at him and not the translator, even though the translator was the one doing the speaking.

This made Aleister uncomfortable. When the translator stopped talking it went dead silent, and the men's gazes then turned back to the translator. The uncomfortable silence went on for what seemed like an eternity to Aleister before the barmaid finally spoke up. "Why don't you come sit down and have a drink?" she said in Norwegian, which the translator relayed to Aleister.

The two of them walked toward the pub's counter. As Aleister and the translator were moving forward, Aleister quietly asked the translator what he'd said to them exactly. The translator said he told them exactly what Aleister had told him to. He told them about the mysterious witch's journal being left on his doorstep back in England and the visit the dark being had paid him. He also told them about his trek to Hammerfest to find answers due to the book having this city's name in it and the fact it was written in Norwegian.

When they both sat down at the counter, the barmaid handed them each a pint of dark ale. She leaned forward and whispered in a very serious tone, "You two aren't looking to live very long, are you? You have no idea what sort of darkness and evil you're getting involved in."

As she spoke, the translator, who was in the middle of raising his glass to take a sip of his ale, suddenly stopped halfway through and froze. Aleister looked over and could see his hand was trembling, causing the ale in his glass to start spilling over the top and onto the pub's wooden floor.

Aleister leaned over and asked, "What did she just say?"

The translator slowly turned to face his employer and replied, "She said we're not going to live long if we continue prying into evil."

"Ask her what she means by that."

When the translator asked her, she began to talk in Norwegian again, and went on for a bit, all the while leaning in very close and whispering so no one else could hear her. As she talked, the translator's face kept getting whiter and whiter until it was as white as a ghost.

When she finished talking and went back to serving drinks and cleaning the counter, the translator calmly set his glass of ale down on the counter, stood up, grabbed his bag, and walked right out of the pub without saying one word to Aleister.

Aleister immediately jumped up and followed him, yelling at him to stop and explain what she'd just said. The translator ignored him and continued walking until he came to the carriage that had brought them to Hammerfest. He walked over to the carriage driver and said something in Norwegian. Then, in an instant, the translator jumped into the carriage and slammed the door shut, all while still ignoring and refusing to even look at Aleister. The driver, who was busy getting ready to leave, quickly scurried to the top of the carriage and sat down in the driver's seat. He grabbed the horses' reins, slapped them on the rumps, shouted something in Norwegian, then took off without saying a word or even looking at Aleister.

Aleister watched as the carriage disappeared into the distance.

LXVI

He stood there in the middle of the muddy road, bewildered, trying to figure out what had just happened. He tried imagining what the barmaid had said to the translator that would spook him enough to suddenly leave as he'd done.

As Aleister stood there, he started contemplating what his next course of action should be. He didn't speak Norwegian, and he wasn't sure if anybody in town spoke English. He knew without a doubt, though, that he couldn't leave until he got the answers he came looking for. He knew the gravity of the situation and how important it was for him to find answers. He knew what was at stake if he didn't.

As he looked around the town, he could see dusk was settling in. It also hit him how quiet and eerie this town was. There was no one else to be seen, and the silence was deafening. One thing he did know was how exhausted he was. He greatly needed to eat and sleep. The long journey had worn him out, not to mention everything that had just happened in the last hour since he arrived. Needless to say, his head was spinning, and the strong alcohol from the ale he drank on an empty stomach wasn't helping the situation.

As he stood there panning around, he spotted what looked to be an inn. He walked over to it, opened the door, and went inside. He could see it was empty except for one man, who was standing at a table cutting up some meat with a large cleaver. The man quickly smiled and spoke to him in Norwegian. Aleister responded in English, saying he didn't speak Norwegian. The man shrugged his shoulders in response. Aleister then motioned to the man that he was hungry and sleepy.

The man said something and motioned to Aleister to sit down at an empty table near where he was cutting the meat. As Aleister sat down, the man walked into the back, disappearing for a few minutes and returning with a plate of food. Seeing a good home-cooked meal brought a smile to Aleister's face. As he sat there devouring his meal with only his thoughts to keep him company, the man continued cutting up the meat.

When Aleister finished his last bite, the man went behind the counter and grabbed a key to a room. He walked back to the table where Aleister was sitting, smiled at him, and handed him the key.

Aleister thanked him and walked upstairs to his room.

When he found his room number, he opened the door and went inside. He put his bag of belongings on the floor, laid down on the bed, and immediately fell into a deep sleep.

That night, as Aleister slept, he had the strangest dream he'd ever experienced. He dreamt he was surrounded in total darkness and could only hear hissing. It sounded like his name was being said over and over again. He was completely helpless and couldn't move his body. He could only turn his head slightly to the sound of the eerie hissing of his name. This went on for what seemed like an eternity, until he was suddenly awoken to the sound of a loud thud coming from downstairs in the inn. Aleister jumped off the bed and ran out of his room to peer down over the balcony. He could see the loud thud had been the innkeeper's cleaver cutting up meat again, and this time it looked like pork belly. He knew what must be for breakfast. The innkeeper looked up at Aleister and just stared at him without saying anything. Then, he went back to cutting up the meat.

Aleister was beginning to think something was very wrong with this little town. He wasn't comfortable being here. He let out a sigh, then turned around and went back into his room. He closed the door and laid back down on the bed.

Even though it seemed to Aleister that he'd slept the entire night, he was still extremely tired and fatigued. It felt like he hadn't slept at all. He laid on the bed for a while, thinking about what his next course of action should be. He knew the first thing he needed was someone who spoke English, even if it was only a little bit. The innkeeper obviously didn't speak any English. They'd mostly communicated through actions and gestures. He decided at that point the best thing to do would be to go back to the pub that he and the translator had visited the day before. He thought there might be a slight chance the barmaid spoke a little English, or at the very least knew someone who spoke English.

He drifted off to sleep again. He wasn't sure how long he'd been asleep before he was suddenly awoken to the annoying sound of a crow cawing right outside his window. As he sat up on the bed, he could see he was drenched in sweat.

He stood up, grabbed a handkerchief from his bag, and proceeded to wipe himself down the best he could. He decided it was time to go check if the pub was open. It looked to him to be well past noon by the position of the sun, so there was a chance he would find someone there.

Just as Aleister was putting on his pants, there was a faint knock at his door, and he immediately froze in place. *Who in the hell would be knocking on my door?*

A few minutes went by as he stood there, frozen, then he heard the faint knock again. This time Aleister gained his composure and finished pulling his pants up. He took a deep breath and went over to the door. Opening the door revealed something far from what he was expecting to see.

There before him stood a strikingly beautiful woman. She had long, silky-smooth black hair that went all the way down to her hips. Her skin was a milky-white color and looked flawless. Her eyes were a deep, dark green, the greenest eyes he'd ever seen. To him, her eyes looked almost like a cat's. After he stopped admiring her beauty and before Aleister could ask who she was or what she wanted, she said, "Hello, Aleister, I've been waiting for you. I take it you got the journal that was left for you on your doorstep?"

Aleister stumbled to find words, having just been hit with another shocking surprise. Not only was one of the most beautiful women he'd ever seen standing before him, but she spoke perfect English. She did have a slight accent, but it was a beautiful, intriguing accent, one he didn't recognize.

"Uh, uh, yes, I got it, and it led me here to this town. Who are you, might I ask?" asked Aleister.

"My name is Asta. I'm sure you have a lot of questions that I may have some answers for. May I come in?" she replied.

"Yes, of course. By all means, come in and sit down," said Aleister as he motioned for her to enter the room.

She walked in, went over and grabbed a chair that was tucked under a small table, and sat down. Aleister noticed as she grabbed the chair and flipped it around, she did so with grace and ease, all without making the slightest sound.

"Aleister," she said, "your reputation in Europe for the occult and dark arts precedes you. I saw you speak to a university class about the occult a year ago in Germany while I was there on business. The rumor now, though, is you're a worshiper and practicer of the dark arts, but, of course, I know otherwise. I know your quest is to stop it. I was, of course, the one who sent the dark witch's journal. You needed to know dark evil exists. There are people who would love to see it enter this world and consume it."

"Who are you, exactly? How do you know this? How did you come across this journal?" asked Aleister.

Asta smiled slightly then replied, "Aleister, what I'm about to tell you, you must never speak of to another living soul in this country. If you do, I will be sought out and burned at the stake, or possibly much worse. I'm a descendant of Mari Jorgensdatter, the witch who was burned alive along with the ten other witches back in 1621 at the Vardo Witch Trials. A little while before she was burned alive for being a witch, she secretly had a daughter, who was taken in by some friends. The family that took her daughter in, my great-great-great grandmother, kept the journal that Mari Jorgensdatter had written."

"So the journal sent to me was Mari Jorgensdatter's?"

"Yes, she wrote it and hid it the night the townsfolk came for her. One thing you should know and understand also, Aleister, is that Mari Jorgensdatter and the ten other women who joined her and pledged their lives to dark evil were not exactly witches. They were trying to be something far darker and more sinister than a mere witch. I myself am a witch, although I am not evil. My acquaintances and I call Mari Jorgensdatter and the ten other women who were burned 'Hexies.' It means, 'powerful evil.' Most people have never heard that word before, and for good reason. The only reason the townsfolk were able to kill Mari Jorgensdatter and the ten other Hexies is because they didn't fully complete their transformation into Hexies. If they'd completed their transformation and had already become Hexies, there would've been no way mere townsfolk could've stopped them. It would've taken someone like you or me."

"Someone like me? What do you mean?" asked Aleister.

"You may not realize it yet, but you're a gifted one. You're on the opposite spectrum of a Hexies. I sensed it when I first saw you in Germany. Haven't you ever wondered why you're so drawn to the dark arts and occult? It's not by chance or mistake you chose this subject to become an expert in. I'm a good witch, which means I can see and sense things most others cannot."

"I always thought all witches were evil, but apparently I was wrong."

"No, not all witches are evil. There are three kinds of witches that exist in this world. A good witch, a neutral witch, and dark, evil witches. I chose to be a good witch when I learned I was a direct descendant of Mari Jorgensdatter. Growing up, I'd always heard the frightening tales about her, but, of course, I didn't know who I truly was, not until I was sixteen years old. When I found out I was her descendant, I knew that was not going to be me. I had to distance myself from her as far as I could because the same blood flowed through my veins," said Asta.

"If you're a good witch, why don't you just stop all of this yourself?" asked Aleister.

"I have been, and I do, but I must also be careful. Since I'm a descendant of Mari Jorgensdatter, that makes me more prone and vulnerable to dark evil, which was part of the reason I became a good witch," replied Asta.

"Well, why don't you just find another good witch to help you?" asked Aleister.

"There are a few who do, but unfortunately, in the world of evil and magic, you don't always know whom you can trust. If that journal were to fall into the hands of an evil witch or another Hexies, the probability greatly increases that the gates would be opened to dark evil, and this world would be consumed by it. That journal tells exactly how to create the doorway to Tenebris and let dark evil in. Some Hexies still know how to create and open the doorway with vague information they've shared with each other over the years, but that journal is an exact roadmap of how to do it. Like I said before, Aleister, you are gifted, and your children and their children will carry the same gift as you. This is something that must be passed down through generation to generation to assure that dark evil is never allowed to enter this realm," replied Asta.

"All right then, what do you want me to do?" asked Aleister.

"Unfortunately, the ten other witches who were burned alive along with Mari Jorgensdatter also had children, and some of them naturally grew up to become Hexies and passed down their darkness to their future generations. However, sometimes others who are not descendants of those ten witches simply appear out of nowhere and become Hexies. I've spent my entire life watching them and waiting, then it has been my duty to kill them. Sadly, my acquaintances and I could not keep track of all of them. Some of them moved outside of the country to seek safe haven from us. I need your help with the ones that fled Norway. They must be killed."

In that moment, it all made sense to Aleister. He could sense what Asta was saying was the truth. He knew what he must do.

"Yes, of course. I'll do it," replied Aliester.

Asta then asked, "You've seen it, haven't you? You've seen dark evil. I can always sense when someone has seen it. They're not like normal people after that. There's always a slight twinge of fear about them. A look of fear in their eyes that never goes away."

"Yes, I have seen it, and it shook me to my very core."

"Then you know the evil we're dealing with, and you will not underestimate it like others have in the past."

"Others? You mean this thing has been here before?" asked Aleister.

"Possibly. The records are sparse, but from what we can gather, ever since man has been alive on this earth, dark evil has been trying to enter our world to consume it," she replied.

"If that's the case, then how has man survived this long without being *consumed* by it, as you call it? You would think they'd have gotten through to our world and overtaken us by now," said Aleister.

"Only because of good witches and gifted ones like you. When Mari Jorgensdatter and the ten other women were burned alive back in 1621, there was a man in this village whose name was Istvan Skarsgård, and he was gifted like you. He didn't know it at the time, but he had the gift to sense evil. He was the reason Mari Jorgensdatter and her companions were discovered. Gifted ones like Istvan Skarsgård and you are the exact opposite of Hexies and dark evil. Without gifted ones, this world would surely perish and fall into the hands of dark evil. I know this all might be a little overwhelming to you, but we haven't much time. Time is always against us."

"How did you learn all of this?" asked Aleister.

"When I was sixteen years old, and after I had decided to take the oath to become a good witch, another good witch came to this village from Oslo. One day, she suddenly appeared behind me and said she had something very important to discuss with me. Luckily for me, though, only good witches have the ability to locate other witches with their senses because she knew exactly who I was and whom I'd descended from. If the wrong witch would've found me first, it could've been disastrous for me. She then sat me down and told me everything she knew. She said it was my duty to find and kill Hexies and to stop dark evil from entering this world. She also said it was my duty to recruit other good witches and gifted ones such as yourself to help in the fight. She became my mentor and my friend, and for the last few decades I've devoted my life to this. Aleister, this was the reason I brought you here. I wanted you to see where it all started. Get dressed. You're going to see the house that Mari Jorgensdatter lived in and was taken from right before she and the other witches were burned alive. I'll also take you to the well their remains still lie within."

"Her house still stands to this day?" asked Aleister.

"Yes, no one has dared touch the house since that fateful night they came and took her. The people who adopted my great-great-great grandmother when she was a baby were the only ones brave enough to venture inside the house to get her things. While they were searching, they came across the journal. They kept it hidden until she was old enough to be told who she was and the truth about her real mother."

Asta then stood up and said, "I'll be downstairs, waiting for you in the restaurant. You should get something to eat before we leave."

LXVI

When Asta left the room and shut the door, Aleister finished getting dressed and gathered his personal belongings. As he was walking down the stairs, he looked over and noticed Asta was sitting calmly at a small table in the far corner. There were several other people in the restaurant as well, and they were all glaring at him in silence as he walked down the stairs and took his seat next to Asta. Asta then spouted off something in Norwegian to the innkeeper. The innkeeper proceeded to walk into the back like the previous night, and within a few minutes he brought some food and a cup of coffee to Aleister. As the innkeeper set down the food in front of him, Aleister realized just how hungry he was.

As Aleister started eating, Asta looked at him and said, "I know we're not very popular here, especially after everyone found out why you were here yesterday. In the future, it's best to keep your mouth shut about anything that pertains to a witch. This village is very leery of anything when it comes to witches. The mere mention of the word can send people into a rage and panic."

"Unfortunately, I found that out the hard way yesterday," said Aleister with a slight grin.

"Finish your breakfast, Aleister. We have a bit of a walk to Mari Jorgensdatter's house."

Aleister quickly finished devouring his breakfast, not because he was anxious to see the house but because he truly was starving. Everything was happening so fast, he didn't have time to think about just how dangerous a journey and path his life was about to take.

Right as he'd taken his last bite of food and sipped his last bit of coffee, Asta said, "Aleister, we must go. Again, time is always against us, unfortunately."

They both stood up at the same time. Asta dropped some coins onto the table, Aleister grabbed his coat from behind the chair he was sitting on, and off they went.

As they made their way down the dirt street, Asta looked at Aleister and said, "Before we arrive at our destination, you must prepare yourself mentally. What you're about to encounter and feel will be similar to the presence of the dark evil you encountered in England."

Right then a chill when up Aleister's spine. He'd hoped he would never have to experience that feeling again. The only comfort he had was knowing this was something he needed to do, and that he was on the right path.

He looked back at her and said, "I understand. I will prepare."

Aleister noticed she was looking directly at him as he spoke, and again, he couldn't help but think just how beautiful she was.

They walked for a while through a thick, dark forest in silence as thoughts raced through his mind. After a while, Asta suddenly stopped and looked over at Aleister and said, "We're getting close now. It's just around that bend. Again, please prepare your mind for what you're about to feel. It's vitally important to never underestimate what we're dealing with."

Alesiter nodded his head, indicating he understood. Asta then continued walking down the dirt path, Aleister following her now.

As they came around the bend, the house and the well where the witches' bodies were buried came into Aleister's view. At that moment, he could again feel the presence of dark evil, the same evil he'd felt before, back in England that night.

As they got closer to the house, Aleister could see that between the house and the well, there was a black octagonal pillar. It was shiny and very black, so black that it almost didn't appear to be real. It was also very clean, which was odd considering everything else around was very old, dirty, and decaying. It looked as though someone had been deliberately maintaining it.

Asta suddenly put her hand up to Aleister's chest to stop him. She looked at him directly in the eyes and said, "Aleister, what I'm about to say is of the utmost importance. The black pillar you see before you is the gateway I spoke of earlier. It's the gateway for dark evil to come through to our world. You must never touch it, even though we believe it's not fully completed. Once it's touched by a human hand, it opens the gateway between our worlds and allows dark evil to enter ours. If you ever give in and touch it, you will be immediately consumed. This is what Mari

Jorgensdatter and the ten other women were trying to complete. Fortunately, they never managed to do so, though the black pillar was somewhat set up. We haven't figured out a way to remove the pillar, as we can't risk a human hand touching it."

"What if a Hexies were to come here and touch the pillar? What's stopping them from doing it?" asked Alesiter.

"Exactly why I need your help to track down the remaining Hexies and kill them. If even one Hexies were to come here and touch this one, or by chance create another black pillar, mankind would be in grave danger. Someone always guards this pillar. I've been watching it for the last several years. Of course, fulfilling that assignment has left me unable to continue tracking down and killing Hexies. The good witch who was guarding this pillar before me had another important journey she had to take, so this duty was passed to me."

"So you just stay out here all the time, by yourself? How do you eat? How do you survive?" asked Alesiter.

Asta smirked and said, "We good witches have special assistants we call trackers. They devote their lives to helping us. In fact, one of my most trusted trackers left the journal on your doorstep in England."

"Where are they right now, might I ask?" asked Alesiter.

"They're always somewhere doing something for us—very rarely are they not on a task. They're also trained to keep a low profile and go unnoticed," replied Asta.

In that moment, Aleister realized with a sense of relief and comfort that he was dealing with smart and tactful people. This made him feel a little bit more at ease, though he knew the dread that very well lay ahead of him.

Aleister noticed the sun was going down, and he wasn't sure if he wanted to be close to the house and pillar after dark.

Asta could sense his uneasiness. "Aleister, what you're feeling right now is actually a good thing. It's that terror and uneasiness that keeps you ready and alert. With what we're dealing with, you mustn't ever get complacent. If you do, you will die. Come, Aleister, I've set up a safe place just behind the house that is guarded with a spell and protected from dark evil."

Aleister continued following her, and as they walked past the black pillar, he tried to look away but couldn't force his eyes to leave it. All kinds of emotions started flowing through him, emotions he'd never felt before. They were the darkest feelings he had ever experienced. The only words he could use to describe what he was feeling at that moment were "pure dread."

Asta took Aleister to a little hut that was about thirty meters behind the house but that still gave them a good view of Mari's old house and the black pillar. As they entered the hut, the dark emotions he was feeling suddenly dissipated, and he started feeling normal again.

Asta turned around with a slight smirk on her face and said, "Aleister, you look like a different person now. You see how important it is to listen to and follow your feelings, for they may one day save your life or the life of someone you care about. Most people disregard their dark feelings and fear as simply being scared or as it being all in their minds, when it is actually evil that is reaching out to them. Evil things do exist. Monsters are real."

"I completely understand what you're saying. My emotions changed once we entered the hut. When we walked past the black pillar, I felt what could only be described as dread and despair, and then those feelings were instantly gone once we came inside," said Aleister.

Aleister noticed there was fresh food on the table and two separate beds in the hut.

"I take it one of your trackers was here today?" asked Aleister.

"Yes, they knew you were coming," said Asta.

"How long am I going to stay here, might I ask?" asked Aleister.

"Until I've taught you everything you need to know to find and kill Hexies. Like us, they know to trust their feelings and can sense when someone on the opposite spectrum is getting too close to them. Someone like you and I, for example. They're very dangerous if you're not prepared, and they're still dangerous even if you are prepared. At least you'll have a fighting chance, though, if you make the proper preparations. They've devoted their entire beings and souls to dark evil and unleashing it into this world, and they are more than willing to die to do so. Like the old saying goes, better to reign in hell than serve in heaven. They'll be sorely disappointed. No human being reigns in the place dark evil resides, which is where they're headed," replied Asta.

"How do you know all this?" asked Aleister.

Asta paused for a moment, looked down, then said, "I've seen it in my mind, at least parts of it. Being a direct descendant of Mari Jorgensdatter doesn't come without its advantages, if they could be called that. Let's eat and get some sleep. I'm sure you're still tired from your long journey. Your mind and body need to be rested."

They sat down and ate dinner, mostly in silence. Aleister was deep in thought, still trying to absorb everything that had happened since the journal had been left on his doorstep. He could sense Asta knew this as well, and she remained quiet, allowing him the time and space to process his thoughts.

It wasn't an uncomfortable silence, though. It was a peaceful, respectful silence. Like old friends who could take comfort just being together without having to fill every moment with words.

Aleister was starting to learn that emotions are just as important as knowledge, and he was learning to trust them. He remembered other times he'd felt strong emotions for something. One time in particular he remembered well was when he first learned about evil and the occult and how he felt about fighting it. Even back then, he felt that he must devote his life to fighting evil. It wasn't until now, though, it all started making sense and he fully understood his purpose. He now knew the gravity of his role in the fight.

After they finished dinner, they had a small cup of brandy to help them sleep. The last thing Aleister remembered was lying down on the bed and staring up at the hut's ceiling. Then, the next thing he knew, it was already morning.

LXVI

He looked over and could see Asta was already awake. She was sitting on her bed across the room, reading a book.

She took notice of him waking and put her book down. "Morning, Aleister. I've prepared breakfast. I trust you slept very well. Anyone who sleeps in this hut enters a state of deep, restful sleep. I imagine it's because this place has been blessed by us good witches. Anyone who enters this hut after walking past the black pillar can no longer deny that good and evil exist. You can feel pure evil and then pure goodness in the same minute. Exactly like you experienced yesterday.”

Aleister knew what she meant because that was what he'd felt the day before. It felt like something that was almost tangible, like he could reach out and touch it with his hand. Words simply couldn't do it justice if you didn't experience it yourself. He thought this must be one reason Hexies were so dangerous. Most people preferred to simply deny real evil exists on the Earth and simply ignore it. Just like Asta had said the night before: evil things do exist, and monsters are real.

Aleister moved over to the table and sat down. He started to eat breakfast, and as he was taking his first sip of coffee, Asta came over and sat down across from him. “Today you're going to learn how to kill a Hexies, before they kill you.”

Aleister almost spat out his coffee. He wasn't mentally prepared to hear it expressed like that.

“Okay, let's get on with it, then,” he said.

“Like I said yesterday, Hexies are like witches but much darker and eviler, which makes their senses much stronger than a mere evil witch. Some are stronger than others, and some can sense you coming long before you see them, which allows them time to prepare before you find them. Once you find them, you must kill them as quickly as you can, regardless if they're in a church or in the middle of town with hundreds of people watching. If you don't kill them quickly, they will most certainly kill you, or worse, they'll flee. They will then find other Hexies, alert them, and possibly join forces,” Asta said.

“So, how exactly do I go about killing a Hexies?”

"This, of course, is the most important lesson you will learn. Hexies have dark evil aiding them, so killing them is not an easy task. It must be done a certain way or they will not fully die. In order for a Hexies to fully die, they must be stabbed in the back of the head with a special blade, severing their occipital artery. The occipital artery supplies blood to the brain. Doing this will kill them in a split second. We're not sure why this is, but it's the only known way to kill a Hexies. Others have tried other methods, failed, and met their fate."

She reached down and picked up the book she was reading. She opened it and showed Aleister a diagram of the human body. She pointed to where it showed the occipital artery that ran up the back of a human's head.

Aleister studied the picture, then asked, "What is this book?"

"It's a book that has been passed down from generations of good witches. It's a compilation of information explaining all of the details regarding Hexies that we have learned over the years. When a good witch learns something new, whether it meets with success or is something that fails, it gets put into this book. Everything you need to know about Hexies can be found within these pages. Unfortunately, it's written in Norwegian, so I must take the time to read it to you. I want you to write it all down in English, so that you can pass it down through your bloodline as well."

Right then it dawned on Aleister he might be one of the few people outside of Norway to know the information he had learned so far, as well as what he was about to learn.

Aleister finished his breakfast and said, "Well, let's get started. We're wasting time."

Asta looked up with a slight grin and said, "That's what I like about you, no hesitation."

The two of them spent the day with her reading from the book and Aleister penning it all down on paper.

The first part talked about how dark evil first came into contact with several women a very long time ago. As was its regular practice, it coerced them into becoming Hexies as a way for dark evil to enter our world and consume it. It also talked about how many times Hexies have tried opening the doorway for dark evil to enter our world only to fail for various reasons. As he was writing, Aleister thought how it would only take Hexies one time to succeed and then the world as they knew it might cease to exist. He also considered the fact that while a lot was known about Hexies, almost nothing was known about the dark evil trying to enter the human world, therefore there was nothing known of how to combat it or stop it if it were to enter our realm of existence. This made Aleister uneasy and even more determined to stop Hexies.

After twelve hours of Asta reading and Aleister writing, they both decided to stop for the day and continue the next day. They ate supper and went to bed.

Aleister again marveled at having slept very well when he awakened. Asta was once again sitting on the bed, only she was reading a different book this time.

Aleister looked at her and smiled. "Do you ever sleep, Asta?"

She grinned and responded, "After you stay in this place for long periods of time and sleep well night after night, your body requires less and less sleep."

They ate breakfast and resumed with Asta reading and Aleister writing.

As Asta started reading from the book, she went into detail of exactly how difficult it is for a Hexies to create a black pillar and open up the doorway for dark evil to enter the human world. One important fact Aleister learned was that two Hexies working together was required to fully create a back pillar. This was one of the reasons it had been difficult for them to succeed and why they had failed so many times.

Once she finished reading that section, she paused and said, "Luck is on our side with that at least, if that's what it could be called. If one Hexies alone could do it, we certainly wouldn't be here today."

"So one could assume that Hexies are constantly trying to find each other, correct?" asked Aleister.

"Yes and no. From what we've gathered, they can't stand being around each other, which is their conundrum. Only when it's absolutely necessary, to fully complete a black pillar for example, do they get together. But more than anything, they desire dark evil to enter our world, which is their weakness."

"Wouldn't they be more difficult to kill if there were several of them together?" asked Aleister.

"Not if you're good and very swift at killing them, and, of course, there are several of us together. Which there must be in that case, and it must be done without any hesitation once they're confronted. A Hexies will never hesitate about killing you once they sense who and what you are. Hesitation is the mother of all mistakes and will cause your worst nightmares to come true," replied Asta.

"Understood. How do I go about finding them? I know you have some names and possible countries they're living in, but won't it still be extremely difficult tracking them down?" asked Aleister.

"Actually, not as difficult as you may think. There are several ways to track them down, and we have trackers on some of them as we speak.

One effective way we found over the years is to listen to stories and rumors from the local townsfolk of witchcraft or evil being practiced. In most cases, those rumors end up being true. They are more than happy to point you in the right direction of the rumors. Hexies can't help themselves when it comes to evil, so horrible things always happen around them, regardless of where they go. Another way to find them is to trust your feelings. That's what brought you here, and it certainly wasn't by accident you arrived. You're gifted, Aleister, and like I said, without your kind or my kind, evil would have consumed this world long ago."

"Good to know, but what about weapons to kill them or how to handle the weapons? I must admit, I've never had to use any kind of weapon growing up, as my family always had armed guards watching over us."

"Do not worry, Aleister. I will train you how to handle yourself and, more importantly, how to use the blades we use to kill Hexies. They're specially designed and are made by a local master blacksmith. We told him what we needed the blades to do, and he designed these specifically for this purpose."

Asta then stood up, walked over to the fireplace, grabbed a wooden box off the mantel, brought it over to where Aleister was sitting, and opened it. "Here is what we call an H-blade. Take it. They're extremely sharp, so be careful. They're cut to the perfect width so they will slice the occipital artery without too much force required. They're not too heavy either, so that you can move swiftly, and they're made of the finest steel known to man. They will never break, as your life will depend on it. Each of us always carries two of them wherever we go. After we finish translating the book, we will move on to your physical training."

As Aleister picked up and held the H-blade in his hand, he couldn't help but admire it. He could see these blades were indeed special, that they were built for a specific purpose. He knew he'd never seen such quality workmanship before, and the steel looked like nothing he'd ever seen.

Aleister put the H-blade down on the table next to him, looked up at Asta, and said, "All right, let's continue moving forward. We have work to do."

Aleister could see Asta was pleased to hear him say that, as a slight grin appeared on her face.

LXVI

They continued for several more days with Asta reading the book aloud and Aleister writing it down in English. Then, one evening, Asta abruptly closed the book, looked up at Aleister, and said, "We're finished. Tomorrow we begin your physical training."

"That, I am glad to hear," replied Aleister.

As he lay there in bed that night, he realized just how much he'd changed in the short time since he'd first come to the hut with Asta. He felt more and more comfortable with what he was doing. Of course, he was nervous about confronting Hexies, as he'd never really had to physically fight anyone, but he knew this was something he must do. He decided in that moment, no matter what, he would never question Asta's training and would focus intently on everything she was going to teach him. He knew his life depended on it.

Morning came, and, as was always the case, Asta was awake before the rooster crows. Normally, Aleister wasn't a morning person, but since he'd been sleeping in the hut, he didn't have a problem waking up and felt more rested than he ever had in his life.

"I've prepared a good, hearty breakfast. You're going to need it," said Asta.

"Good, I'm looking forward to it. I've never had to even think about learning how to fight, but I am very interested in learning now," Aleister said.

"I have no doubt you will excel at it. Keep in mind, though, that all the knowledge in the world won't save you from a Hexies. It will be your body's reflexes and how swiftly you move that keeps you alive. If a Hexies gets the upper hand on you for even a second, you're dead."

Hearing those words made Aleister even more diligent. He quickly ate breakfast, then followed Asta outside behind the hut. Asta had come outside earlier, while Aleister had been sleeping, and set up what appeared to be a scarecrow, which was meant to mimic a person. There was a rope attached at the top of the scarecrow and one attached to the bottom, so it wouldn't swing out of position. There was also something to the side of the scarecrow that looked like a throwing board with a target in the middle of it.

"Aleister, most of your training will be on what I believe in English is called a scarecrow. First, though, I will teach you how to wear the H-blade and how to handle the H-blade properly. After that, I will teach you how to use it to slice the occipital artery in less than a split second. Every second is of grave importance, as you have less than a second to make your kill strike."

Aleister nodded his head, showing that he understood and took what she said seriously.

"Your H-blade must be positioned on your belt in the middle of your back, for two reasons. The first reason is so that as you walk, you can keep both hands behind your back without drawing suspicion because, as you know, aristocrats usually walk with both hands behind their back. This means you must always dress and act as an aristocrat to look the part. The second reason is so you have it drawn well before you approach the Hexies, in case they sense you and try striking first. In such an event, you would not have time to reach behind your back to draw your H-blade, unless, of course, you're extremely lucky or circumstances outside their control permit it. Better to be prepared than unprepared. Hexies very rarely allow for a second chance. Always remember that, Aleister."

Again, Aleister nodded his head in acknowledgment. Asta then opened a black case that contained two H-blades and two beautiful-looking sheaths. Each sheath had Latin inscribed on them that read: *deditio optio non est,* which translates to, "surrender is not an option." Aleister knew this because he'd been studying Latin since he was very young.

"These two H-blades are yours, Aleister. Guard them with your life," said Asta as she laid them on the table along with a brown leather belt.

"Take care of them and they will take care of you. Each blade is always blessed by a good witch. These two were blessed by me. Give them the utmost respect, as they are without a doubt the sharpest blade you'll ever handle. Once you lose respect for them you will injure yourself, and the consequences can be severe. I've watched people who didn't respect them lose fingers with the slightest brush up against the blade. Part of your training will be how to quickly extract the blade from your sheath without injuring yourself. I will demonstrate and explain how this is done correctly, several times, of course, before I allow you to attempt it yourself. Losing one or more of your fingers would make you slow, and therefore useless against a Hexies."

Asta turned around so Aleister could see her H-blades and she could show him how to correctly draw them. He could clearly see the two H-blades she had strapped on her belt in the middle of her back, an inch apart from each other. Her H-blades looked almost identical to his, except the Latin on her sheaths read, *nulla misericordia,* which translates to "no mercy."

"Always grab your first blade with your dominant hand. It must become muscle memory, and consistency is the key. You will perform exactly as you practice. Even the simplest mistake or quirk made over and over again will carry over into your performance once the time comes. It must always be, no matter what, the exact same. I will demonstrate slowly at first, so focus on every movement I make, as well as the angle of my arm and wrist and the position of my fingers as I grip the blade."

Asta demonstrated multiple times, moving ever so slowly in order for Aleister to catch the slightest details of her actions. She didn't have to worry about him focusing. It was safe to say this was the most focused Aleister had ever been on anything up to this point in his life. He knew his life depended on him performing these steps perfectly, and he was determined not to fail in his assignment.

"Aleister, now attach your H-blades to your belt as I have and practice drawing them, ever so slowly at first. I will watch your technique and critique as necessary," said Asta after she had demonstrated the proper form several times.

Aleister stepped up to the table where the belt and black case holding the H-blades were sitting. Before reaching out and grabbing them, he sat there admiring the quality workmanship of the blades. He'd never seen blades like this before. They were incredibly beautiful. He looked over at Asta, who had a slight grin on her face. He could tell she knew exactly what was going through his head.

Damn, she's clever and *beautiful,* he thought.

He then lifted the sheath out first, as it made sense to take things slowly in the beginning. He picked up the first H-blade and was amazed at the weight. It felt perfect. Not too heavy but not too light either. He slowly slid the first H-blade into its sheath and then did the same with the second one. After that step was completed, he slid them both onto the brown belt she'd given him. Lastly, he attached the belt to his waist just as Asta had with her own.

"Not bad, Aleister. I can see you pay attention to detail," Asta praised him.

Hearing that was good for his confidence. This was all very new to him, and all he had to go on was what Asta taught and told him. He realized that might actually be a good thing, as there were no old habits to break. *I'll be taught the correct way from the start,* he thought, feeling another boost in his confidence.

"Aleister, first you must practice drawing the H-blade as I did, over and over. Always respect the blade and be mindful of it. Everything you do must be a conscious action and effort. The moment you become complacent and lose focus is the moment—how do you say in English?—shit happens. We will start with you very slowly drawing the H-blade so that I may watch each detail of your technique. Then, once I'm satisfied with your performance, you'll need to go grab your coat and practice with it on. Like I said, you need to be dressed as an aristocrat, and aristocrats are always wearing a jacket. Another perk to that is a jacket conceals your H-blades. Again, you'll perform exactly how you practice because of muscle memory. Drawing an H-blade while wearing a jacket is very different than when not wearing a jacket. I wasn't wearing one because I wanted you to be able to see every step of how to properly draw the H-blade."

Aleister nodded his head, indicating that he understood. He turned around so his back was facing Asta and began practicing drawing his own H-blades. The first few times Asta said nothing, but on the fourth draw,

she stopped him, critiquing his technique, though managing to do so
without criticizing him, only telling him what he needed to change.

After several hours of practicing drawing the H-blade Asta told him to go
get his jacket. He was ready to take his training up a notch. Aleister
nodded his head, went and grabbed his jacket from the hut, then came
back to the exact position he'd been practicing. As he put his jacket on,
he could tell in an instant that it was going to be very different. He also
realized without Asta helping him he would've never thought to wear his
jacket while practicing. He would have continued on without it, which
could have led to serious trouble for him in the long run. He knew a small
detail like that could spell death for him when the time came to meet a
Hexies face-to-face.

He spent hours, well into dark, practicing drawing the H-blade with his
jacket on. Just when he thought his arms would give out, Asta said,
"Aleister, let's stop for the day. We'll pick up where we left off
tomorrow, and we will also practice with you walking while drawing the
H-blade. You will almost always be walking swiftly as you approach a
Hexies to make a kill, with your hands behind your back, and like I said,
your H-blade must be drawn long before you approach a Hexies to make
a kill strike."

They both went into the hut, ate some bread, and Aleister downed a jug
of water. Soon after that Aleister crashed on the bed from exhaustion. It
was a good exhaustion, though. He liked the way the training made him
feel.

LXVI

Morning came fast, and he was awoken to the wonderful smell of
bacon frying.

After breakfast they went out to the practice area. Asta stood by and watched as Aleister strapped on his H-blades. He spent the day practicing over and over again, drawing the H-blade as he walked. As he was practicing, Asta stressed making as few movements as possible with his arms. She said to make it seem as if his arms weren't moving at all, until he was ready to strike, to let his hands do all the work under the jacket. "The less attention you draw to yourself, the higher chance of success you have," she reminded him repeatedly.

"Hexies are highly suspicious of everyone and everything around them. If they catch you staring at them for too long your chances of success decrease dramatically. Too much attention focused on them will do nothing but put them on high alert," she said.

"When you stab a Hexies in the artery, it must be a complete and utter surprise. You walk up behind them, draw your H-blade, stab them in the occipital artery, and then continue walking without missing a single step—one fluid motion. You have to keep in the mind also that normal people don't know what you are, or what a Hexies is, so it'll look like murder to them, should they happen to witness your actions. You must always be discreet and never get caught. The last thing you want is to get arrested. If you perform the task fast enough, no one will notice what took place. The Hexies hitting the ground, dying instantaneously, will be the first indication of anything being wrong."

Aleister nodded his head, acknowledging he understood. It was starting to get dark by now, and he was extremely tired. He'd lost track of time and actually couldn't even remember what day it was. All he knew was that he was starving.

Asta, being astute as always, said, "Come, let's eat, then go to bed. We will resume your training in the morning. You're exceeding my expectations, Aleister."

The next morning was the same as it had been since he arrived. He awoke to Asta's beautiful face, with her sitting on her bed reading a book and breakfast already prepared and waiting on the table. Aleister did notice he was gradually waking up earlier and earlier as each day passed.

After they finished eating breakfast, Asta said, "You're ready to move on to the scarecrow today, which happens to be where the rest of your training will resume from here on out."

Aleister took the last sip of his coffee, slowly put down his cup, and felt a sadness creeping over him. He knew he was getting closer to the day when he would have to leave here. He'd been enjoying his time with Asta, and he was thinking about the fact that the chance he might not see her again caused him great sadness. He sat there for a moment, not saying a word.

As if she'd been reading his mind, Asta said, "If I can help it, Aleister, this won't be the last time we see each other. There's always some form of communication every time you kill a Hexies, as we keep strict records of all slain and living Hexies. Our paths will surely cross again, that I promise you."

Aleister felt a slight sense of relief hearing her say that. "Good," he said with a smile. "Let's get started with today's training, then!"

Aleister grabbed his H-blades that he now kept next to his bed, then grabbed his jacket and followed Asta outside the hut. When they got about halfway to the scarecrow, Asta turned around and said, "I want you to walk over there and stand exactly three feet from the scarecrow, off to the side, so that you can get a clear view of what I'm about to demonstrate. I'm going to show you how to perform a kill strike on a Hexies. This is the most important lesson you'll learn with the physical training. Pay attention to every single move I make, as each move, no matter how small, has a specific reason behind it."

Aleister walked over to the exact position Asta told him to stand, waiting with his hands behind his back. Asta took about ten steps back, then proceeded to walk swiftly with her hands behind her back like she'd taught him. As she got closer, Aleister was extremely focused on her arms, checking for movement, but he could see none. He noticed her eyes were not fixed on the target but to the side of it. Obviously, you don't want to be staring directly at a Hexies as you're walking toward them, when the goal is to move in without being noticed.

When she was about one stride away from the scarecrow, Aleister saw her eyes change, and she focused on the back side of the scarecrow's neck. What happened next looked like a quick flash of movement, with her right arm coming up and hitting the back of the neck so quickly he barely had time to register the movement before she calmly continued walking as if nothing happened. It was poetry in motion, graceful and beautiful. Aleister looked at the neck of the scarecrow and could see that there was a perfect horizontal cut right where the occipital artery would be located. He almost started clapping but stopped himself for fear of looking like a fool.

He couldn't hide the smile on his face, though, and when Asta turned around she saw him smiling, and she smiled right back and said, "I'm glad you enjoyed it, Aleister, I've spent many years perfecting it. I'll do it several more times, and this time try focusing on other aspects of my body that you didn't focus on the previous time. Again, each and every movement has a purpose behind it—how many steps I take, when I pull out my H-blade, where my eyes are focused, how straight my back is. I think you get the idea. You want to match your movements and strikes as closely to mine as possible."

She proceeded to do it several more times, each demonstration seeming identical to the very first one. Aleister would focus on a different part of her body each time she repeated it, watching each and every detail. He started visualizing himself doing the exact same thing.

After several more times Asta turned to Aleister and said: "All right, Aleister, it is now your turn. I'll be watching closely and critiquing as needed."

Aleister walked over to the exact position where Asta had started, took a deep breath, and ran over the movements in his mind to push out the nervousness he was feeling. He then started walking and moving exactly how he'd been taught by Asta. When he was one stride away from the scarecrow, he pulled the H-blade from its sheath and let it fly, focusing intently on the area where the occipital artery would be located if the scarecrow were a real person. As he hit the neck of the scarecrow, he could see he hit the occipital artery perfectly. He resheathed his H-blade and calmly continued walking.

A sudden rush of adrenaline swept over him. He immediately wanted to do it again and again.

He turned to face Asta, who was smiling. "Aleister, you are a quick learner. There's a reason you are who you are and why you're gifted. I only noticed a few mistakes that will be easily corrected through repetition. We will continue practicing this every day for several more weeks, until it's second nature to you."

That was music to Aleister's ears. He knew how important it was to perfect the art of the kill strike on a Hexies, not only to save himself from being killed but for mankind itself.

Aleister spent the rest of the day practicing over and over again, hitting the scarecrow in the neck. With each strike he became more and more confident in his abilities. Asta stood there watching him each time, not saying a word, which in Aleister's mind meant he must be doing it correctly.

This intense practice went on day after day for several more weeks, until Aleister started having dreams about it at night. It was then he knew it was instilled in his brain and was becoming second nature. Asta told him to always continue practicing, even after he left Norway. She told him he must never lose his edge, as it could easily result in losing his life. She also told him to keep his body in peak condition and to never become overweight or obese.

As they were eating dinner one night after a long day of practicing, Asta put down her spoon, looked up from her stew, and stared at Aleister for a while before speaking. When she did finally speak, she said, "Tomorrow you will leave on your journey. It is time for you to start killing Hexies." She then picked up her spoon and continued eating her stew.

Aleister didn't say anything. He had known this day would come and had been expecting it. He wasn't sure exactly how long he'd been with her at the hut, but it seemed like months. He knew it was time to leave. As she had told him again and again, time was always working against them in this fight.

They went to bed a little while later without saying a word, maybe because they'd come to enjoy each other's company and parting ways was going to be difficult. Maybe it was because there was a chance they wouldn't see each other again, and they both knew that was a real possibility.

Aleister awoke the next day as he had every day since he arrived, with Asta sitting on the bed reading a book and breakfast on the table. Today was different, though, and he could feel it. There was an air of sadness between them that didn't need to be mentioned or shown; it could be felt by both of them. From Aleister's observation, Asta was a master at self-control, never showing too much emotion. Thinking back to past women he'd had relationships with, he felt that was a rare quality for a woman. Her very survival required her to be strong emotionally and physically, and that's what he admired most about her. He knew she was special, unlike any woman he'd ever encountered or might ever encounter again in his life.

They ate breakfast in silence. After they finished, Asta walked over and squatted down on the wooden floor in the corner of the room. She opened up a secret compartment underneath the floorboards and pulled out something that was hidden for obvious reasons.

"Aleister, this is a map of all of the Hexies and their last known locations. As you kill a Hexies, it is imperative that either you or the tracker notify me by letter. One of my trackers will intercept the letter in Hammerfest and bring it to me. Also, please keep me updated as to what country and city you're in, if possible. Hexies sometimes change their locations suddenly, and I will need to be able to reach you if that happens."

"How do you even keep track of these Hexies and actually know which cities they're in?" asked Aleister.

"Our trackers are tasked to locate them like we talked about before, based on information from local townspeople. They then keep tabs on them, from a distance, of course. Our trackers are very skilled at what they do. However, they are not gifted or trained as you and I are, and if they approach a Hexies alone they will certainly be killed. Since we don't know each Hexies' real name, the trackers assign each one a name of their choosing. We then mark each one down on the map here, along with their location."

Asta then laid out a large map of Europe on the table in front of Aleister. He could see names in several different countries, some of which had an X through them. He assumed an X meant they'd been killed.

"There are sixteen active Hexies in Europe that we know of right now. More, of course, can always come into the fold, but luckily for us, they're usually very careful and slow to recruit. If they recruit the wrong person and the local townsfolk find out, it can spell death for them. No matter how strong a Hexies is, it can't physically stop a large number of people. One other important thing we must do is to stop them from reaching America. It would be a very difficult task for our trackers to find them there. It's a rather large country, as you know, and none of our trackers have ever been there, so their capabilities would be severely limited in that environment," she said.

As Aleister was continuing to look over the map, Asta said, "I'm going to assign you five Hexies to track down and kill. You will be given the tracker's name in each case, along with the city they're in. You will then meet up with them, they will show you the Hexies they're keeping tabs on, and you two will formulate a plan to kill them. One word of advice: always listen to what the trackers have to say. Some of them have been tracking and following these Hexies for months or longer. They can give you critical insight into the Hexies you're targeting. Keep in mind also that at the end of the day, a Hexies started out as a normal human being, so each one is different, with a different personality and level of intelligence. The more you know about your enemy the better edge you'll have."

Asta grabbed a piece of paper and a quill pen. She began to write down the names of the Hexies, and next to each name, she noted the country they were in. More importantly, she wrote down the address and name of the tracker who was assigned to each Hexies. When she was finished writing, she handed the paper to Aleister, who took it and began reading over the names and locations.

He noticed the Hexies were in Denmark, Poland, Germany, Italy, and Greece. So many different countries. This was not going to be easy. He knew he had a long journey ahead of him.

He sat there for several minutes, looking at the paper and trying to find any last words he wanted to say to Asta. Before he could speak, Asta said, "I know, Aleister. It's hard to find the words. I promise we'll see each other again. Let's get your things ready; it's time to leave. You may have to spend a day or two in Hammerfest, depending on when the next stagecoach comes through."

Aleister stood up from the table and started to gather his things. As he was packing, a lot of thoughts were running through his head. He thought about Asta, unsure of what was going to happen next. He knew his first destination was going to be Denmark, being it was the closest country to his current location, and it made sense to start there.

LXVI

When he finished packing and turned around to walk toward the door, he could see Asta waiting by the door with something in her hand. As Aleister walked closer, he could see it was a letter that looked like it was sealed with red wax that had been stamped with what looked like a ram's skull.

Asta reached out and handed it to Aleister. "Open this one year from today and not a day early."

They walked outside together and headed toward the trail that led to Hammerfest. As they passed the black pillar, Aleister was again overcome with a sense of dread. He remembered how different the hut felt from the black pillar, and also Mari Jorgensdatter's house, which still gave him quite an uneasy feeling as he passed it.

They walked side by side along the trail that led to Hammerfest without saying much. They were both deep in thought about the future and what was going to happen.

Asta had known all of this information since she was sixteen years old, but Aleister was still trying to wrap his mind around everything.

It hadn't been too long ago that he had been in England living in his family's mansion in the lap of luxury, but now here he was headed to Denmark to hunt and kill a Hexies. Knowing full well his own life would be at stake if he made a mistake was a major shift in perspective.

As they walked along the trail to Hammerfest, he kept replaying his training in his mind. He would go through each step slowly, to be sure he would not miss a single detail.

After a few hours of walking they came out of the thick forest. He could see the village of Hammerfest in the distance, and he knew it wasn't long before they would reach their destination.

Asta turned to Aleister and said, "When we get there, I'll find out when the next carriage leaves for Oslo. From there you'll need to take a boat to Copenhagen, Denmark, to meet up with the tracker."

"I understand," replied Aleister.

When they made it to Hammerfest Asta walked into the stable and spoke to a man in Norwegian, then turned to Aleister and said, "We're in luck. The next carriage for Oslo leaves in a few hours, and there's room for one more. Let's go get lunch and talk before you leave."

They went to the inn where Aleister had stayed when he first arrived in Hammerfest. Things felt different now as he walked inside. He had more confidence and was more aware of his surroundings than he'd ever been before. He looked at people differently than he used to, not as nuisances or enemies but as friends. He almost sincerely pitied them, knowing most people would never know what was going on behind the scenes of "normal" life. They were oblivious to what would happen if dark evil managed to find a release into the world.

They sat down at a table, and Asta ordered lunch. As they were waiting for their food, Asta started asking Aleister personal questions. This was something she'd never done before, and it took him by surprise.

"Aleister, what was life like for you, growing up in England?" she asked.

"I actually come from a fairly wealthy family. We own one of the largest breweries in England. I admit, life was fairly easy growing up. However, this did give me the opportunity to study or do whatever I wanted. As you know and mentioned before, I took a keen interest in the occult and dark magic, against my parents' wishes, of course. I would read and absorb any information I could find on the subject. I mean, I even went to other countries so I could study it. Of course, you know that already, having seen me speak in Germany on the subject. I knew the occult and dark magic was something that could be dangerous, but I wasn't sure how dangerous until the journal arrived on my doorstep. It was then the pieces of the puzzle started to fit."

"You are correct. It can be dangerous and devastating, unless people like us stop it. One other thing I wanted to discuss with you is the tracker you'll be meeting in Copenhagen. Each tracker is a different person and, naturally, has a different personality, so it's always good to know a little bit about the person you're going to meet beforehand. Take out the paper with the tracker's name on it."

Aleister reached into his satchel and took out the paper that had the location of the Hexies and names of the trackers. He now took the time to actually look at the name of the trackers, having just glanced at it before. He read the first name aloud, "Hans Meyers."

"I've known Hans for a number of years. He served as my tracker here in Hammerfest for quite a while. He's a brave and loyal man, and you can trust him with your life. He's also easy to get along with and will follow your every command. Do not forget, it's important for you to listen to him as well, as he's been following the same Hexies for over a year now. He will know details about the Hexies that may prove vital to you successfully killing them, and, of course, to your own survival."

As Asta finished her last sentence their lunch arrived. They made friendly conversation as they ate, simply enjoying each other's company.

When they finished eating, Asta looked at Aleister and said, "It's time to go. Your carriage leaves soon."

Aleister had known this moment was coming and hadn't been looking forward to it. He stood up, grabbed his satchel, and made his way to the door as Asta followed.

They walked in silence toward the stable. Aleister could see the driver of the carriage was loading up luggage and preparing to depart. The driver then turned, put his hands up to his mouth to make himself heard better, and shouted something in Norwegian.

Asta turned to Aleister and said, "He said the carriage for Oslo leaves in five minutes. I guess this is goodbye, Aleister. I look forward to hearing from you soon."

Asta extended her hand, and Aleister looked at it for a minute before he extended his own. "It's been quite a pleasure, Asta," he said as he shook her hand. "I truly look forward to the day we meet again."

Aleister turned and walked toward the carriage. He handed the driver some money, then climbed aboard and took the first available seat. As he turned to look out the window of the carriage to see Asta one more time, he realized she was nowhere in sight.

LXVI

He sat back in his seat and let his mind begin to wander. He was thinking about the journey he was about to embark on, and everything that had transpired since he'd left England. He could never have imagined he'd be in the situation he was in today. Sitting in a carriage in Norway, getting ready to track down and kill evil, still seemed surreal to him. Somehow, though, he felt comfortable in what he was doing, and he knew what needed to be done. If not him, then whom?

Right then the carriage driver climbed aboard and sat down. He shouted something in Norwegian, slapped the reins on the horses, and off they went, headed for Oslo.

It was a long journey, just like he remembered when he first came to Hammerfest. They would stop every few hours for breaks and to eat something. Aleister slept a lot as the carriage made its way to the big city. His brain was worn out from having to learn and absorb so much during his time with Asta.

After several days the carriage finally pulled into Oslo and stopped. The driver shouted something in Norwegian, which Aleister assumed meant they'd arrived. He couldn't remember being more grateful. Spending several days in a cold, bumpy carriage without anyone to speak to in English was not his idea of a good time.

Aleister quickly grabbed his bags and headed toward the boat harbor.

His plan was to meet up with Hans in Copenhagen at disembarkation. The thought of killing someone, even if they were pure evil, still hadn't sunk into his mind yet. He kept telling himself, *It's either them or us,* and he had to admit, he preferred the former.

As he made his way to the ticket booth to buy a ticket, he was thinking about Asta and what she might be doing at the moment. He figured she was doing something important, as everything she did seemed to have a purpose behind it. He couldn't remember her ever wasting a single minute while she was awake during the time he spent with her.

He bought his ticket to Copenhagen from the booth that was directly in front of the ship he was to board. It was scheduled to leave within the hour, so he immediately boarded the ship and found a comfortable seat where he could sit by himself and gather his thoughts. The boat ride to his destination would not be long. He felt this was a good thing, as he was tired of traveling.

As he sat there waiting for the ship to leave, his mind wandered deep into thought. When he came to, the ship was already well on its way and sailing along. He hadn't even noticed when they'd set sail and left the port, which was usually quite a noisy process. As he was sitting there, his stomach began to growl, and he realized how hungry he was. He couldn't remember the last time he had put anything in his stomach, even a drink of water. He stood up and headed toward the kitchen to get some food and hopefully a pint of beer. As he walked into the kitchen area, he noticed other gentlemen drinking beer, and that put a smile on his face. He wanted to relax as much as he could before arriving in Copenhagen, and a pint of beer was exactly what he needed.

He walked over to the bar and ordered some food and a pint of beer. He then sat down in the corner of the kitchen area to enjoy his meal and beer by himself. After he finished eating, he must've dozed off again because he was awoken to the sound of the ship being docked. He noticed the bar and kitchen area was completely empty, except for two barmaids who were quietly wiping the counter and mopping the floor.

He jumped up, grabbed his satchel, and headed for the door. He wasn't sure how long he'd been asleep, and Hans was most likely waiting for him on the dock. He didn't want to start out on the wrong foot with the other man. He knew how important Hans was in what they were doing. He also knew that his very life could be in Hans's hands.

As Aleister walked down the plank to the dock, he noticed a man with dark black hair who looked to be in his thirties, standing about fifty yards to his right, looking directly at him. He could see by the way he was looking at him that it must be Hans. Aleister approached the man, and when Aleister was within about fifteen feet, the man put up his hand and said, "Stop right there. What is your name, sir?" Aleister stopped, looked around to see if anyone was near them, and said in a low voice, "My name is Aleister Crowley. Might you be Hans Meyers?"

The man replied in a serious, emotionless tone. "Yes, sir, I am Hans Meyers. Asta's letter said you'd be coming, but I just wasn't sure which day exactly. I've been coming here for the last two days. So you're the one I've heard so much about. If you're as good as she says you are, we might just live through this," said Hans.

Aleister waited for Hans to crack a smile after he said that, but it never came. Again, Aleister reminded himself this was serious and not a game.

"Come, let us go. We have much to discuss about the first Hexies you're going to kill. Like Asta might have said to you, time is always working against us," said Hans, his face never shifting from the fiercely serious expression Aleister had first noted.

"Where are we going?" asked Aleister.

"To the place I've been living since I arrived in Copenhagen. The place you'll be staying as well while we're here. We'll always stay together, so we can watch each other's backs. Hexies are obviously smart, and they are very dangerous. They will never let on they know they're being followed until it's too late. Now that you're here, things will change."

Aleister followed Hans from street to street until it had been dark for what seemed like hours, until they came to a small five-story building. They made their way around to the back of the building. Once they were at the back door Hans started to pan the surrounding area, even looking above them before entering the building.

Once inside, Hans shut the door and turned to Aleister. In his thick German accent, he said, "Never just quickly walk right in without checking your surroundings. Hexies are all about ambushing you. When we get to our room, I will show you how to check to see if a Hexies has entered while I was gone."

Aleister then followed Hans as they slowly climbed up the five flights of stairs. Aleister could see that Hans was very cautious. Even as they crept up the stairs, it was as if Hans was expecting someone to be hiding and waiting to attack them from somewhere in the dark.

When they finally made it to their room, Hans again looked around for anything unusual. He took something small and black out of his pocket. It looked almost like an arrowhead. He started moving it along the door, in an upwards and downwards motion.

"This is a talisman that has been passed down through generations of good witches. It will turn white if a Hexies is near, or if a Hexies has touched our door in the last few hours. It's not changing color, so we're clear to enter."

Aleister had been carefully observing since he first met Hans. He wanted to know everything and wasn't leaving any detail to chance.

Inside the room they would now share, Aleister immediately noticed all of the strange things that were scattered about. It was almost as if he'd stepped into another world. The windows were blacked out, and all kinds of strange trinkets were hanging from the ceiling. There were also some strange, almost disturbing drawings on the walls.

His attention soon turned to the center of the floor. In the center was a great big black circle that had been drawn with what looked like charcoal paint. In the middle of the circle was a black painting of the skull of a ram. He thought that he'd seen this painting somewhere before but couldn't remember exactly where. With everything that was happening over the last few months, it was easy to forget or dismiss some seemingly unimportant things.

Hans looked over at Aleister, who noticed he was looking at the painting on the floor, and said, "This circle is the only thing that will keep you safe from a Hexies, besides the hut you stayed in with Asta. They are not permitted to enter it, therefore we always sleep inside the circle, and for good reason. I imagine you have many more questions about many of the things you see throughout this room, and we will talk about some of them when the time comes. It's getting late, and we try not to venture too far after dark. Hexies' source of power comes from darkness, which means they're much stronger and more alert at night. I've already prepared our dinner, so we'll eat and discuss the Hexies we have to kill in this city. Come, please sit down."

Hans walked over to an old black stove that had a large black cast iron pot sitting on it and lifted the lid.

Whatever it was, it smelled good to Aleister.

"Are you good with eating venison?" asked Hans.

"Yes, as a matter of fact, I love venison. Used to eat stag all the time back in England," replied Aleister.

"Good, cause venison is a good, clean meat. It's good for our senses, so we'll be eating it frequently. I'm not sure if you're aware of this or not, but anytime you consume the flesh of an animal, some of its senses are passed on to you, be it good or bad, so we always eat clean meat. We must have heightened senses at all times," said Hans.

This was the first time Aleister had heard this, but it made sense to him. He would happily comply, as he wanted to do whatever he could to give himself an edge.

Hans reached up and grabbed two bowls from a cabinet above the stove. As Hans closed the cabinet, Aleister noticed the cabinet had an interesting and very detailed carving on it. One side of the cabinet had a carving of a beast that resembled a demon, with outstretched wings and claws coming out of the tops of the wings. The other side of the cabinet had what appeared to be a knight of old holding a long spear aimed at the demon. They looked to be battling each other.

As Aleister was looking at the cabinet, Hans appeared to crack a slight smile.

"The demon or beast, whatever you want to call it in English, is what some believe dark evil looks like. However, no one can be absolute, as no one has seen it in the flesh and lived to tell about it—as far as we know anyway. Only in its transparent form. That cabinet has been passed down for many years, as have many of the items in this room. Every item in this room has a purpose or it would not be here."

After Hans finished stirring and heating the stag stew, they sat down in the black circle and started eating. It had been a while since Aleister had a nice home-cooked meal, and this delicious stew was long overdue. He savored every bite as the tender venison literally crumbled in his mouth.

Once they finished Hans took both bowls, went over to a sink that was next to the stove, and immediately washed them. Once clean, he put them back in the cabinet with the carvings on it.

"We always put everything back in its place as soon as we're finished. Right now, though, we need to talk about the Hexies we're going to kill," said Hans.

"Good, man. I want to know every detail, big or small," said Aleister in a serious British tone.

"The Hexies we're going to be killing is a female, and I've given her the name of Klug. It means clever in German. I've been watching her for quite some time, and if there's one thing I've learned about her, it's that the name Klug fits her very well. She's also as skittish as they come and is strikingly beautiful. I'm telling you that last part so there is zero hesitation when the time comes to do what needs to be done. Don't think for a second that she won't gut you from groin to eyeball if she senses you. As I've followed her, I've seen her do things to people that would make your toes curl. Unfortunately, all I can do is watch, as I'd very well be next if I intervened, especially if she knew I was following her. I'm not gifted like you are, and as you know, it takes a gifted one to slay a Hexies."

"Anything else I should know about her?" asked Aleister.

"Yes, she's constantly looking over her shoulder and has excellent peripheral vision. It's been very challenging for me to follow her and go unnoticed. There were a few times I thought without a doubt she noticed me. I must have been wrong, though. Otherwise, I wouldn't be sitting here today. Hexies won't hesitate for a second to kill someone they think might pose a threat. She does have one weakness that could well prove helpful."

"And what might that be?" asked Aleister.

"She has a weakness for currant berries. She buys them in large quantities several times a week. We might be able to use that to our advantage."

"Currant berries, huh? Interesting. Yes, that is something we might be able to use to our advantage," Aleister agreed.

"Tomorrow, I will show her to you. Then we'll spend another few days watching her so you have a good idea of what you're up against. Then we'll discuss what's going to be the best strategy for killing her," said Hans.

Aleister simply nodded his head in acknowledgment.

The rest of the evening was spent mostly in silence. After an hour or so, Hans brought out two bed rolls and blankets and laid them down in the middle of the circle. He explained to Aleister that it wasn't a good idea to leave the circle after the candle went out and the room was dark.

"Make sure that you take care of anything you may need before I blow out the candle, so that you can remain inside the circle. If a Hexies somehow manages to get inside this apartment and catches you sleeping outside the circle or wandering outside the circle for any reason, it will most certainly spell instant death."

Aleister nodded his head that he understood. For the first time since he'd left Norway, chills went up his spine.

They both readied themselves for bed. Hans then brought a candle with him into the circle and said, "Aleister, I'll always let you know right before I blow the flame out." He then blew it out, and the room was overtaken by a heavy silence.

LXVI

Aleister was awoken the next morning by Hans gently grabbing his shoulder and saying, "It's time to wake up, Aleister. We have a very busy day ahead of us, and I like to catch Klug out early before it gets too busy. It's easier to follow her if there's less people in the streets."

"What exactly does she do all day?" asked Aleister as he stood up and stretched.

"She's like us in the fact that she has to earn an income to survive, even though her quest in life is to release dark evil into the world," replied Hans.

"What does she do for work?" asked Aleister.

"She works at a brothel, believe it or not. With her looks, she is quite popular among the men in this city, based on the rumors I've heard. It's actually a smart strategy, in case she needs to use men for help. I imagine she has more than enough men willing to do anything for her. This also allows her to hide in plain sight without raising much suspicion," replied Hans.

"Smart, beautiful, and deadly. That's a dangerous combination," said Aleister.

"Quite right, quite right," Hans agreed.

They ate a quick breakfast that consisted of some type of Danish bread and eggs.

They then quickly changed their clothes and readied themselves to head out into the city. Aleister made sure he properly mounted his H-blades onto his belt just in case. He didn't forget what Asta said about always carrying them, no matter what.

As Hans opened the door to the apartment, he ever so slowly stuck his head out and looked all around before setting even one foot outside.

"We're clear," he said as he moved forward.

As they walked down the hallway toward the stairwell, they did things as they had the day before, slowly and cautiously. When they made it outside, Hans picked up the pace, with Aleister trailing behind him.

As they walked along the cold streets of Copenhagen, Aleister took note of every street and every building, in case, God forbid, something happened to Hans and he had to come back to the apartment alone. He knew the black circle with the ram's skull was the only safe haven and could save his life.

They'd been walking for about thirty minutes when Hans suddenly stopped right before going around the corner in front of them.

He turned around to face Aleister and said, "We're not too far away from her place now. It's around the corner and down the street a bit. We must keep somewhat of a distance, so she doesn't sense your presence. A word of advice, Aleister, do as I do—mimic me as much as possible. I will try to move slowly without drawing attention so my actions will be easy for you to follow."

Aleister nodded his head in agreement, having remembered what Asta said about having the advantage of surprise.

Hans then motioned to Aleister to peek around the corner and said, "She lives down the street a bit on the left-hand side. When she leaves the building, she will head down the street toward her work, so we will follow and stay back as far as we can. She should be leaving any minute now."

Hans and Aleister stood there waiting a few more minutes, then Hans whispered, "All right, let's move. Remember, though, mimic me, and always walk on the side of me. We need to be having a conversation like we're old friends. Never, ever look directly at her. I will describe her to you, but I will also never look directly at her."

Hans then started casually walking down the right-hand side of the street as they rounded the corner. Hans was looking at Aleister as he was walking and started describing her and where she was at exactly. "You see the woman about four blocks down on the left, wearing a black silk dress? She has long blonde hair that's almost down to her buttocks?"

"Yes, I see her," replied Aleister.

"Good, now continue talking to me. It takes her about fifteen minutes to walk to work, and we're at a good, comfortable distance right now. I want you to watch her closely out of the corner of your eye and see how she moves and reacts as she walks. Today, her hair is let down, but most of the time it's pulled up in a ponytail, which makes her peripheral vision much better. Again, she is clever. I think it's best if you wait to strike on a day that her hair is down," said Hans.

"I agree. Good observation, Hans," said Aleister.

Hans and Aleister continued walking down the street and talking. They would only take quick glances out of the corner of their eyes as they walked. Aleister paid especially close attention to how often she would take quick glances to the right and to the left of her. He could see exactly what Hans was talking about. She was indeed skittish and would not be easy to sneak up on.

They followed her for about ten minutes before Hans said, "Let's take a left here. She's almost to work, and we don't want to walk behind her for too long. I usually take position from a distance on rooftops or from vacant rooms, so that I'm completely out of her sight. If I was to follow her every day she would most certainly notice me, but today, I wanted you to see her place and get a close look at her."

"I can see why you felt that was a necessary first step. She's very alert and looks like a coiled cobra, ready to strike at any moment," said Aleister.

"Exactly. I'm glad you noticed that. That's exactly how she is. Come, let's go back to her apartment building and go inside. There's something I want to show you, and it's good to get familiar with where she lives. Don't worry, she won't come back and catch us. In the time I've been watching her, she has never come back to her apartment early after going to work," said Hans.

"I'll follow your lead," said Aleister.

As they walked back to her apartment building, Aleister noticed Hans was very carefully but nonchalantly checking his surroundings. He never let his guard down, even though he was confident she would not come back. This made Aleister feel comfortable and more confident in trusting Hans.

When they got to her building Hans walked right in without missing a step. Aleister assumed he wanted to blend in, appearing as if he actually belonged there.

When they got inside, Hans looked at Aleister and said, "She lives on the third floor. We'll go to her door, and I'll show you what I need you to see."

They walked up the stairs, remaining cautious as they arrived on the third floor. As they were approaching her door, Hans reached down into his pocket, just like he had the previous night, and took out the arrowhead-looking talisman. As he was taking it out of his pocket, Aleister could see that it was white as snow on Christmas Day, completely opposite of the color it had been when he used it near their own door the night before.

"This is what happens when a Hexies is near or has been near recently. It senses evil," said Hans in a whisper.

Hans had barely finished speaking when Aleister sensed something was behind him. As he turned around, he saw a flash of something. Before his brain had time to register what was going on, Aleister could see Hans being lifted into the air and pinned up against the wall. Klug's long, black claws were clutching his neck. Aleister could see blood starting to trickle down his neck. In that same instant, without thinking, Aleister grabbed his H-blade from behind his back. Instincts took over. He went into action without hesitating, slicing her occipital artery within seconds, and the next thing he knew, Klug's body was hitting the floor.

Hans also fell to the floor on all fours, coughing and spitting up blood as Aleister stood there without moving. Adrenaline surged through his body as his mind struggled to register what had just happened, and the fact that he'd just taken a life.

A few minutes went by before Hans was able to gain his composure. When he did, he sat up against the wall, clutching his neck. When he could finally speak, he said, "She must've sensed your presence and come back. She obviously didn't know you were the gifted one or you'd be dead, since she was behind you first. She guessed at which one of us she thought was gifted and guessed wrong. We sure got lucky this time. Next time we'll keep more distance between us and them. No one knows exactly how close a gifted one can get to a Hexies without them sensing you, and each Hexies has different skill levels."

"Hans, as soon as you're able, we need to leave this building. We cannot risk someone seeing us and Klug's body together. The last thing we need is the authorities arresting us."

Aleister reached down and helped Hans stand up. Once the other man was on his feet and he was able to get a closer look at his wounds, he realized how close Klug had come to ripping out his throat. His wounds were dangerously deep. He looked down at Klug, who was lying on her side in a pool of blood, her eyes wide open. He could now see what Hans meant; she truly was beautiful. Strikingly beautiful, in fact, just like Asta. The pool of blood around her was growing, and he knew it was time for them to leave. They didn't want to risk getting blood on the bottom of their shoes and walking out of the building, leaving tracks of blood as they walked.

They hurriedly went to the building's exit as Hans did his best to walk on his own. He struggled to maintain a decent composure, trying not to draw attention to them. Before they exited the building, Aleister handed Hans a scarf that he had in his satchel.

"It would be wise to cover up your wounds so they don't draw unwanted attention, and it will have the bonus effect of helping stop the bleeding as well," said Aleister.

LXVI

Once they exited the building, Hans went into cautious mode once again and scanned the area before departing.

The walk back to the apartment was a struggle, to say the least. Hans was bleeding quite a bit, and he was in an immense amount of pain, so much so he had to stop himself multiple times from vomiting on the street. Once they did make it to their apartment's door, he again pulled out the talisman and scanned the door to their apartment. It remained black.

Once inside, Hans instructed Aleister on how to mend his wounds. Aleister grabbed the first aid supplies Hans had in a cupboard and mended his neck as best he could, considering it was his first time. Hans then collapsed onto the floor in the middle of the black circle and fell asleep from exhaustion and loss of blood. There was nothing more Aleister could do. Left alone with his thoughts, he could only hope his new ally would survive. It wasn't as if he could call a doctor, as it would draw too much suspicion. Klug's dead body most certainly would have been discovered by now.

Aleister became lost in his thoughts of what had taken place that morning. He was still in shock. The events replayed in his mind as if set on repeat. He kept seeing her beautiful face frozen in a death mask, as a pool of her own blood spread around her.

Aleister must've dozed off himself because he was awakened the next morning to Hans shaking him out of his slumber. Aleister jumped up in fright, wondering what the hell was going on.

"It's okay, Aleister, you're safe in the circle. You may have nightmares for a while. The gifted ones always do after each kill."

"I did have the strangest dreams last night. I can't even describe them because they don't make sense to me at all," Aleister said, struggling to control a shudder.

"I believe that. Your mind might be a bit different now, and you will have nightmares for a while," said Hans.

"Hans, where do we go from here?"

"Well, what I was instructed to do if we were successful was to travel down through Denmark, then cross the border into my home country of Germany. The sooner we can leave this city the better, in fact. The authorities will be searching for Klug's killer now."

"Do you have any information about the Hexies we're supposed to kill in Germany?" asked Aleister.

"Not much, only an address and the name of the tracker we're supposed to meet up with," replied Hans.

"What's the tracker's name, might I ask?" asked Aleister.

"Of course. His name is Dolph Gruber, and he's in the city of Bremen. I've never been to Bremen, so this should be interesting."

"When do we depart?" asked Aleister.

"In a day or two, at the latest. I need to rest and heal up some more before we move. I'm also going to send word to Dolph that we're coming, so he'll be expecting us."

Aleister could see Hans was in a great deal of pain. He was handling it as well as anyone could be expected to, though, judging by the deep, nasty wounds on his neck. Aleister could still vividly recall watching Klug's arm getting ready to pull back and tear Hans's throat out in the same second he was slicing into her occipital artery. If he would've hesitated a fraction of a second longer Hans wouldn't be sitting here with him today.

A serious expression came over Hans's face as he looked at Aleister. "Thank you, Aleister, for saving my life yesterday. I am forever in your debt. I will never forget it."

Aleister nodded his head in acknowledgment and said, "Of course, Hans. You would've done the same for me."

The next two days were mostly spent inside the apartment, with Hans resting and educating Aleister on everything he knew about Hexies. He also talked about the various objects in the apartment and the purpose of each one. This fascinated Aleister a great deal because there were so many things he had never known existed, even though he'd been studying the occult and dark magic for many years. It was like he was in another dimension altogether. He thought most people wouldn't believe their ears if they heard what Hans was telling him.

When Hans felt well enough to travel, they loaded up what they needed and left for Bremen. They traveled by train, as it was faster and much more comfortable than a horse and buggy. The journey by train would be much better for Hans, who was still in a significant amount of pain and preferred to avoid the bumpy ride a horse and buggy would provide.

After an uneventful seventeen-hour train ride, they arrived in Bremen, Germany, during the night hours.

As they grabbed their bags and were stepping off the train, Hans said, "Dolph should be meeting us at the ticket booth over there." Aleister just nodded his head and followed Hans as he led the way to their designated meeting place.

As they approached the ticket booth, they saw a man standing there, staring at them. He was wearing a brown tweed hat, a long, black leather jacket, and he had a fairly big red beard. He was standing calm and composed with his hands behind his back.

When they were several feet away from him, he spoke to them in English and asked, "Are you gentlemen Hans and Aleister?"

Hans replied, "Yes, we are, and you must be Dolph?"

"Yes, I am, it's a pleasure to meet you two. Hans, I hope you don't mind if we speak in English so that Aleister doesn't miss anything important?" asked Dolph.

"Not at all. I agree with that. I also wouldn't want to alienate him from our conversations," replied Hans.

"Thank you both for that. I think it's also a good way to keep less ears from understanding our conversations if they happen to overhear," said Aleister.

Dolph and Hans both nodded their heads in agreement.

"Well then, let's grab your things and make our way to the apartment before it gets too late. We have about a twenty-minute walk from here," said Dolph.

"Agreed," said Hans.

Hans proceeded to tell Dolph everything that had happened to them in Copenhagen with Klug. As Hans told the story, Aleister noticed that Dolph's face didn't change one bit. He kept his composure, even when Hans told him the details of how close he came to having his throat ripped out. Aleister was becoming more impressed with these trackers the more time he spent with them. *This must be one reason they were selected for this task,* he thought. A normal person wouldn't be able to handle the stress of their life being in danger at all times.

After Hans finished the story, Dolph said, "That's good information to know. I think we should keep a good comfortable distance from the Hexies we're going to kill. Aleister may be very gifted, which might make it easier for them to sense him—perhaps that is what went wrong for the two of you. I'll tell you the details of the Hexies we're going to kill once we're inside the apartment."

Just as Hans had done in Copenhagen, when they arrived at their destination, they went around to the back of the apartment building, Dolph switching into cautious mode.

They followed the exact same procedures as they entered the apartment building. This time, though, the talisman that Dolph took out was shaped like the antlers of a red stag deer. Thankfully, when Dolph used it to check the door, it remained black instead of glowing white. A sense of relief came over Aleister. He was tired from traveling and was not in the mood to deal with another Hexies this soon.

As they entered the apartment, Aleister saw that it looked similar to the one in Copenhagen. It also had the black circle with a ram's skull in the middle of it. The only thing that was different were the trinkets and items that were placed throughout the apartment.

After Dolph closed and locked the door, he looked at Hans and Aleister and asked, "I trust stag steaks and red potatoes are all right for dinner?"

"That'll be perfect. Thanks, Dolph," replied Hans.

"That sounds splendid to me as well," Aleister added, remembering what Hans had told him about venison.

The consistency he saw between these two made Aleister feel good, and he guessed trackers must be trained exactly the same way. He appreciated that knowing that would mean he knew what to expect when changing assignments, and there would be less surprises from one tracker to the next.

After putting their bags in the corner of the room, Dolph served up their dinner. They all sat down in the black circle as they ate, just like Aleister and Hans had done in Cophenhagen. As they ate, Dolph gave them the details about the Hexies they would face in Bremen.

"This Hexies is a female, like the one you killed in Copenhagen. Most of them will be female because of the nature of the beast—the dark evil and what it's after and what it craves. I named this one *Gefährlich* or *Fährlich* for short, which translates into dangerous in English. I gave her that name for two reasons. One, so I never underestimate her, and two, because she is quite dangerous. More dangerous than the one you encountered in Copenhagen I would dare say. Fährlich is older and much more experienced than Klug, from what Hans has said."

"In what ways, specifically?" asked Aleister.

"She's been around for quite a while, and she simply has a lot more experience than Klug. She moves residences often, which makes her harder to track. This means she most likely knows she's being watched, or at the very least she's suspicious that she's being watched. From what I've been told, she knows a lot about both trackers and gifted ones. And lastly, she trains a lot in combat, so she's sharp and on edge all the time. Think of her as three Klugs tied into one."

"If that's the case then we most definitely need to keep a comfortable distance between her and us. We can only get close when it's time to strike. I'm also going to need your help to kill her," said Aleister.

"Of course, Aleister, whatever you need," said Hans.

"Certainly," Dolph added.

"Good. Let's come up with a plan then, and I'm open to ideas. Especially from you, Dolph, as you know her best after tracking her for so long."

"Yes, of course. I'll start contemplating some ideas," replied Dolph.

They mostly sat in silence the rest of the evening, until it was time to go to bed. Just like in Copenhagen, Dolph brought out some bedrolls for them along with a candle, this one black. He blew it out when it was time to sleep.

LXVI

When Aleister awoke the next day, he had no idea how long they'd been asleep. He looked over and saw Dolph sitting at the table, reading a book. Hans was still fast asleep.

Aleister stood up and walked over to Dolph, who whispered to Aleister so as not to wake Hans, and said, "I figured I'd let you both sleep late, considering what you've both been through, especially Hans. His body is still healing and needs the rest. Sit down here, if you don't mind, as there's some important information I need to cover with you."

Aleister nodded his head as he sat down by Dolph at the small wooden table.

"Tonight, after she comes home, I'm going to show Fährlich to you and Hans. Obviously, this will be done from a good distance. We'll actually be using a telescope to watch her. Now, I'm still not sure what she does for a living. I've been watching her for four months, and she eludes me every morning, and I do not see her until she comes back at night. I'm only able to keep tabs on her on the weekends. During the day, though, it's a total mystery to me, which is concerning. Like I mentioned yesterday, I think she knows someone is watching her, or she always assumes someone is watching her. Either way, she is going to be tough to kill. I've been thinking about what you said last night, about needing our help, and I've come up with some ideas of how you can get close to her."

"Good, let's hear them," replied Aleister.

"Of course, we should strike her on a weekend, when I know her habits best and the streets will be crowded. This will help us when she senses you because she won't know exactly who the gifted one is—she will only sense your presence. She's obviously not going to just start attacking people at random. No, she'll wait until she knows for sure who the gifted one is, then she'll strike hard and fast. Of course, we aim to prevent that and kill her first. She goes to the market for food on the weekend, and I think it would be best if we strike her when she's in the middle of paying for her food, so that her hands and mind are preoccupied, if even for a few seconds, at least until she senses you. You'll have to move very quickly once you decide to strike because the second she senses you she'll be on high alert. Hans and I can get somewhat close to her and watch her before you strike, giving you some sort of a signal, because she can't sense us. Another advantage we have is, there's no possible way she's seen my face, and Hans has never been to Bremen before, so he's even more of a stranger to her than I would be."

Right then Hans chimed in, "I like it. I think it might actually work. Sorry for jumping in. I was awake long enough to hear your idea, Dolph."

"Not at all, Hans. I'm glad you heard so I don't have to repeat myself. Any other ideas you can bring to the table would be much appreciated," replied Dolph.

"Sounds like a good plan to me. I'm going to err on the side of caution and assume she'll be able to sense me long before I get close enough to her. With you guys keeping a close eye on her, I'm hoping that will give me a slight edge," said Aleister.

"Then it's settled. Let's eat lunch, then I'll take you to the spot I watch her from. We'll spend at least a week or more watching her if need be before we strike. By the way, how are you feeling, Hans?" asked Dolph.

"Much better now that I've gotten some rest. I should be good to go with you guys after lunch."

"Good to hear. I've got lunch cooking on the stove. We're having stag stew," said Dolph.

Hans wasn't kidding when he said they eat a lot of stag meat, Aleister thought. Again, it was consistency and discipline, and Aleister found comfort in it.

Dolph served up their lunch in some old wooden bowls that he pulled from a cabinet similar to the one Hans used in Copenhagen. This one had different carvings on it. The carvings on this one depicted a half demon-half horse on one side, throwing a trident at a person dressed in a black cloak with no face showing.

Again, they all sat down in the black circle and ate their stag stew in silence. Each one was deep in thought about what was going to happen when the day came that they would approach Fährlich face-to-face to try to kill her. They knew just how dangerous she was and that this day could very well be their last spent on Earth.

After they finished eating, they all stood up, gathered their things, and followed Dolph outside. They walked for about an hour to the spot Dolph had been using to watch Fährlich. It was on top of a tall building, which had a clear view of Fährlich's apartment and a clear view into her room.

As they sat down, Dolph said, "We're almost two kilometers away, so I'm hoping that's far enough she doesn't sense you, Aleister. If she does sense you, any element of surprise we had will be gone when we attack, or worse she disappears."

Dolph pulled out his pocket watch to check the time and said, "All right, gentlemen, she should be coming home in about ten minutes."

Dolph then reached down and opened up a case that he'd been carrying. As he opened it, Aleister and Hans could see what looked to be a high-quality telescope nestled inside.

"How good is that thing, Dolph?" asked Aleister.

Dolph replied, "Good enough to see what she's eating for breakfast. When she decides to keep her curtains open, that is. She is very elusive and secretive, as most Hexies are. Every once in a while, I get a ten-to fifteen-minute window of time where she leaves the curtains open, and even that seems rare nowadays. Sometimes she'll come out on the roof of her apartment building and just sit there for an hour or so."

"What does she do on the roof?" asked Hans.

"She does nothing but sit. It looks to me like she's mediating, because her eyes are closed, and her hands assume a meditative position. I can only imagine what she's meditating about, but she may in fact be praying to dark evil. Either way, she's always striving to get closer to her goal of opening the doorway to dark evil," replied Dolph.

Dolph finished setting up the telescope as he was talking. He then aimed it toward her apartment building, adjusted the focus, then started slowly moving it around for several seconds. In a calm, clear voice, he finally said, "Here she comes, right on time. Aleister, you be the first to look, since you're the one tasked with killing her. We only have about a five-minute window until she reaches her apartment building, then it's a gamble on whether we will get another chance at seeing any more of her today. If you look now, she's the only one in the telescope. She's wearing a black cape, and she has hair that is as black as charcoal."

Dolph quickly moved out of the way, allowing Aleister to sit down and look through the telescope. What Aleister saw sent chills up his spine. She did look and act differently than Klug. Fährlich seemed much more confident as she walked, like she wasn't afraid of anything. She didn't look behind her and didn't act skittish—she acted like a predator. She also seemed to have a very dark aura around her. She was not beautiful nor was she ugly; her face seemed "normal." Nothing made her stand out like Klug's striking beauty had. This would make Fährlich more dangerous. She could blend in easier and disappear. He now understood why Dolph had chosen to name her "dangerous." If what he saw and thought was true, then this Hexies was very dangerous.

After a few minutes of watching her, Aleister moved and motioned to Hans to come and take a look. Aleister was at a bit of a loss for words and just sat down against the roof's brick wall to absorb what he'd just witnessed. A lot was going through his head in the moment—fear and doubt, but also courage and strength. He knew there was no other option but to kill her. Again, the same thought he had before ran through his mind: *If not me, then whom?*

As Hans was looking through the telescope, he said, "Well, she entered the apartment, so I guess we'll see if we get lucky and she makes another appearance. She is exactly as you described, Dolph. Aleister is probably thinking so as well. I can certainly see why you named her Dangerous. She is going to be a difficult one to kill. I would venture to say her range on sensing a gifted one reaches quite far, and she'll be on high alert well before we lay eyes on her. We'll definitely need to pick a crowded street, and I would also say we may need some more eyes positioned above us to help signal us if she decides to make a run for it. We don't want her leaving the city, or worse, the country. We'll need every advantage we can get if she decides to stay and fight, which I'd bet she will choose to do. She may try hunting you down first, Aleister, once she senses you. We must be prepared for several different scenarios."

Hearing that didn't make Aleister feel any better, but again, he thought, *If not me, then whom?*

Hans then moved so Dolph could take over the telescope and hopefully catch another glimpse of her. They sat there for another two hours, mostly in silence, until it was almost dusk, but she never came back out or opened the curtains to her apartment. They could only see her room lit up from behind the window coverings.

Once the sun set behind the mountains, they all immediately stood up, gathered their things, and didn't hesitate, leaving as quickly as they'd come. They knew what darkness brought, and they weren't going to sit around to find out if Fährlich had already sensed Aleister. Nothing was left to chance when death was on the line.

As they walked down the streets of Bremmen, they hurried along as quickly as they could. There wasn't any sense of relief until they were all inside the apartment and close to the black circle with the ram's skull.

Dolph made a delicious German dinner of potatoes and stag bratwurst. This was something Aleister had actually been wanting to eat since he arrived back in Germany. It had been a while since he was in Germany and had an authentic German bratwurst. He had learned to take joy in the small things since this journey started some months ago. He was starting to miss the comforts of his home and his family.

LXVI

As they were sitting in the black circle, eating, Aleister looked over at Dolph and asked, "Dolph, my friend, what's our plan for tomorrow?"

"I was thinking we'll wake up early tomorrow morning so we can catch her leaving her apartment. Hopefully you'll have longer than a five-minute window to watch her. The more you watch her, the more of a sense you'll get about her. You can learn a lot by simply watching someone."

Aleister knew this to be true, having seen just how different Klug and Fährlich were simply by the way they walked down the street, their movements, and their facial expressions.

After they finished dinner and cleaned up, they all sat in the black circle. They talked for several hours about each other and what their normal routines were like before they committed their lives to finding and killing Hexies. It was a way to take a break mentally for what was to come. The conversation went from laughter and reminiscing to sadness as Aleister learned about Hans and Dolph and their lives before all of this. They had both been regular men, working to put food on the table and living normal lives—that was until both of their wives and kids were viciously murdered by Hexies. They'd both set out for revenge against the Hexies who killed their families, but luckily, they were stopped by a good witch who took them in and explained what would happen if they approached a Hexies on their own. The good witch trained them and taught them a better way to get revenge. So, for the last ten years, they'd both been tracking Hexies alongside gifted ones, doing their part to kill as many as possible before their own lives came to an end.

Neither Hans nor Dolph had dry eyes after they told Aleister their tragic story. They told him in detail how their small children were taken and killed as sacrifices for the sake of dark evil. It was hard for Aleister to fully understand the pain of losing a child, as he'd never had a child himself. He could only imagine the pain and anguish they must feel daily. He did see the passion in their eyes as they spoke, and how they both said they would lay down their very lives to kill as many Hexies as possible, if only to spare any other child the fate their own had suffered.

The next morning they awoke at five, so they would be sitting in position when Fährlich left her apartment to go wherever she went every day. They ate a quick breakfast of bread and sausage and hurriedly left under the cover of darkness. As they walked along the cobbled streets of Bremen that crisp early morning, none of them spoke. Instead, they were each on high alert and very mindful of their surroundings. It was still dark outside, and Hexies were at their strongest in the dark.

They made it to their position atop the roof. They huddled down to get out of the bitterly cold wind that was blowing that morning. Dolph quickly took out the telescope and got it into position. They could see lights were coming on all around them, as people were waking up for the day. Dolph took aim with the telescope, and after a few minutes, he whispered, "Her apartment light is on, so she should be leaving very soon. Aleister, come here and sit."

Aleister didn't hesitate, quickly taking his place in front of the powerful telescope. Within a few seconds Fährlich's light went out. A minute later she came out of the front door of the apartment building, paused for a moment, looked both ways, turned left, then calmly started walking down the cobbled street. She walked exactly as she had the day before, dangerously calm and confident. Aleister watched her until she turned a corner and was out of sight. He couldn't help but wonder where she would go every day, for hours at a time. This really started bothering him, like a sliver in his brain. He couldn't shake the feeling that whatever they were missing would jeopardize their mission somehow.

Aleister looked at Dolph and said, "We must find out where she goes every day."

"I thought you were going to say that, and I agree. It is something we must know before we strike. I've been thinking up a plan, and now that Hans is here and there are two of us trackers, I think we can manage it," said Dolph.

"Good man. Let's hear your plan, then," said Aleister.

"I propose that tomorrow morning, when she leaves her apartment, Hans and I simply follow her together, side by side, like we're old friends headed to work. We're fairly certain she knows a lot about trackers, and anyone that knows anything about trackers knows they're solo most of the time. So with there being two of us and the fact she hasn't seen either one of us before, she shouldn't have any reason to suspect us. We'll, of course, keep a safe, comfortable distance, and if at any moment we feel she suspects we're following her we'll immediately vacate the area. I also think we should disguise ourselves somewhat, so when the time comes to kill her, she won't recognize us. What do you gentlemen think?" asked Dolph.

"I like it! Simplicity is sometimes best. With the two of you together, which is rare like you said, this gives us the advantage," replied Aleister.

With a slight grin on his face, Hans nodded his head in agreement.

"Sounds like a plan. We'll come back tomorrow morning, and the two of you will follow her as I watch from the telescope. I'm sure I don't need to tell the both of you to be careful. If she catches on she's being followed and decides to lead you down a dark alley, you'll certainly be killed," said Aleister.

Hans and Dolph both nodded in agreement with somber looks on their faces.

"Please use good judgment, as I can't afford to lose either one of you, and to be quite honest, I've grown to like and respect the both of you. Let's go back to the apartment and prepare," said Aleister.

They grabbed their stuff and left the rooftop. As they were leaving, they could see a storm in the distance, brewing in the sky, which seemed fitting, as they knew they might be creating their own storm the following day.

The rest of the day and evening was spent discussing all of the possible scenarios of what could take place if they were discovered by Fährlich. They planned for the worst but hoped for the best. They were trying not to leave anything to chance.

The next morning they awoke at 4:00 a.m. to eat an early breakfast and to go over every possible scenario again. This also allowed them to prepare mentally for what might happen.

Hans and Dolph didn't try lying to themselves when it came to the real possibility something could go horribly wrong. Truthfully, though, a small part of them always longed for death, so they could see their wives and children again. The biggest part of them wanted to stay on Earth long enough to rid the world of as many Hexies as they could, but there was no denying the smaller and no-less-real part of them.

They left the apartment building around 4:45, giving themselves plenty of time to make the walk to Fährlich's apartment. They needed to be in position well before Fährlich left her building.

The plan was for Hans and Dolph to wait five blocks from her building. Then, when she left, they were to simply follow her, hoping she didn't decide to turn around and take notice of them, or worse, head down the street toward them. They knew she was smart, but there was no way of knowing just how smart. They were all more than aware that bumping into her a second time could prove to be fatal.

Hans and Dolph had both decided to shave the previous night, significantly changing their appearances, since they had both had full beards. They planned on growing them back before the day came to kill her. Hopefully this would change their appearance just enough.

As they stealthily walked along the streets of Bremen in morning darkness, heading toward her apartment building, all three of them were silent.

Aleister split off from Hans and Dolph when the time came, heading toward the building and the rooftop he would watch from, with the telescope in hand.

There were a lot of thoughts running through his mind as he walked that cobblestone street alone, moving toward the apartment building. He wasn't sure what was going to happen, since, in all the time he had been following her, Dolph had never gotten so close to Fährlich before. Aleister did his best to keep a positive outlook, but this game was entirely new to him. He hadn't even known what a Hexies was until he met Asta. Hans and Dolph, on the other hand, had been doing this for over ten years. He could only imagine what was going through their heads at the moment, after all of the horrific things they had seen during their decade of service.

Aleister finished picking his way through the street to the apartment building, then went up the ten flights of stairs to the rooftop. Once there, he unpacked the telescope and hurriedly got it settled in the preselected position. He didn't want to miss anything. He knew he'd only have about a five-minute window to watch her and them. When he got the telescope aimed at her apartment building, he could see the light was already on. He released a sigh of relief, realizing this meant she was still in her apartment.

In that same split second, the light to her apartment went off. Aleister knew she would appear at the front door very soon, so he quickly moved the telescope to point down to her apartment building's front door. She soon appeared in the doorway, and like before, she paused for a moment. While she stood there, Aleister kept repeating in his mind over and over, "go left, go left" because Hans and Dolph were behind her to the right. Ten seconds went by, and she finally turned left. That was the longest ten seconds of Aleister's life. He felt his stomach start to churn—he couldn't help but wonder why she'd paused for so long. He followed her with the telescope as she walked down the street, keeping his eye on her until she was out of sight. He then moved the telescope back to watch Dolph and Hans.

Soon after, Hans and Dolph appeared in the telescope, walking along the cobblestone street. And just like they should be, they were casually walking and talking like old friends as they followed behind Fährlich.

Aleister knew they would be out of sight within a few minutes, and then it would be an intense game of patience, waiting for them to return. The plan was for Aleister to go back to the apartment and remain in the black circle until Hans and Dolph returned. If they didn't return by the following morning, he would know that they were both dead. If that happened, Aleister was instructed to travel down to Hanover, Germany, to meet up with another tracker, then they would come back and finish the job.

When Hans and Dolph disappeared from sight, Aleister didn't waste any time grabbing his things, hustling off of the rooftop, and heading back to the apartment. When he made it inside the apartment, he quickly grabbed some water, bread, and some leftover sausage before moving to do as he had been instructed. He sat down in the circle and planned on remaining there until they returned, or until the following morning, when it became obvious that they would not be coming back. He made sure all of his belongings, including his H-blades, were inside the circle.

LXVI

He remained in the circle all day with nothing but his thoughts. He tried pushing the negative thoughts out of his mind, thinking instead about Asta and his training during the time that he spent with her. He wasn't sure of the exact time he dozed off, but he remembered being jolted out of his slumber to the clicking sound of the door being unlocked and opened.

The door creaked loudly as it was being opened, and instinct took over, causing Aleister to jump up and reach for his H-blades. He quickly drew them from their sheaths a second before he recognized Hans and Dolph as they appeared in the darkness, slowly creeping through the doorway. Their hands were raised, and they were motioning to Aleister as they whispered, "It's all right, Aleister. It's us."

"Good God, you guys scared the hell outta me! What time is it, anyway?" asked Aleister.

"It's just past 3:00 now," replied Dolph.

Aleister lowered his hands, put his H-blades back into their sheaths, and said, "Boy, am I ever glad to see you two. I wasn't sure I'd ever see you again. Well, what the hell happened? What did you see? Don't keep me in suspense."

Dolph replied, "Aleister, let's sit down. We have much to discuss."

They then sat down inside the black circle as Dolph gave a detailed account of everything that had happened during the course of their day.

"I'm sure you watched us through the telescope until we disappeared, correct?" Aleister nodded that he had. "After that, we had a very difficult time keeping up with her without getting too close. She took many turns as she walked through the streets of Bremen. She must've walked for two hours before she finally came to the edge of the city. She then made her way to the outskirts of the city, to the beginning of Westliche Forest. This is where things got really tricky because there's a big wide-open field between the edge of the city and where the forest starts. We certainly couldn't follow her as she walked through the open field, as she would've most certainly noticed us. At this point we noticed that she did start looking behind her, to make sure she was not being followed," said Dolph.

"So, what happened?" asked Aleister.

"We quickly ducked inside of an apartment building on the edge of town and looked out from the third-story stairwell window. We needed to get a bird's-eye view of where she was going. Then, we waited until she entered the forest and made a mental note of the exact spot we had last seen her. We waited for twenty minutes before we left the apartment and set off following her again," replied Dolph.

"Once you got to the spot where she entered the forest, how did you continue following her if she was out of sight?" asked Aleister.

Dolph looked over at Hans, who then looked up at Aleister and said, "I've been a hunter all of my life. My father taught me how to track animals very well through almost any environment, especially a forest. Once we made it to the place where she had entered the forest, it was just a matter of finding her footprints—slight disturbances in the dirt, broken twigs, or crushed leaves. Luckily for us, though, the ground was somewhat moist, so she left footprints that were visible enough for us to follow easily. This also allowed us to see where she was going ahead of time, before we had to walk. So we could take our time and creep along very slowly, observing the area and what lay ahead of us before we would get there. If she caught us off guard in the forest, we knew we would be dead before we even had a chance to realize what happened."

Hans then lowered his head, and Dolph took notice of this, speaking up to continue their account of what they had experienced. "We then followed her tracks for several hours. That is, until we came to where we could see a small clearing about one hundred eighty meters ahead of us. It was then that a very dark feeling came over us, so we instantly took cover behind some deadfall. We could feel her presence in the clearing, and we knew we had to somehow get a good look into the clearing without being detected. After a few minutes of whispering back and forth about the best way to proceed, we finally decided. We belly-crawled for fifty meters to the best vantage point we could find. It was then we saw her in the middle of the clearing, kneeling down. Luckily for us, she had her back turned to us as she was kneeling down."

Dolph then paused for a moment to gain his composure.

"We could see something in front of her. It was black and shiny, and we instantly knew what it was. It was a black octagonal pillar. We assumed, though, she must still be waiting for another Hexies to come and help finish creating it, otherwise she would have already opened the doorway. She stayed kneeling in front of the pillar for several hours, without moving a muscle. All the while, she was chanting something over and over again in Latin. We never could make out exactly what she was saying, only that it was Latin. We stayed in our position until she finally left, praying to God she wouldn't walk past us on her way out.

"When she did finally stand up to leave, the hairs on the back of our necks stood on end. All we could do was sit there in horror, waiting to see which way she was going to go. Once again, we got extremely lucky. She walked just to the left of us about ninety meters. We laid there behind that deadfall for another thirty minutes before we got up and slowly walked out of the forest. It's safe to say that from the time she left the black pillar until we got back to the apartment were the longest hours of our lives. We had no idea what was going to happen to us. Would we get lost in the forest? What if she was waiting behind a tree to pounce on us at any moment?" said Dolph.

"I can only imagine," said Aleister.

"Knowing that a black pillar is already set up, we now realize it's only a matter of time before another Hexies comes to join her and the final steps are completed. The doorway to dark evil will then be opened. We must move quickly and kill her at once. If dark evil is unleashed into this world, there's no way of knowing if it can be stopped," said Dolph.

Aleister knew from the moment Dolph mentioned seeing the black pillar they would have to kill her very soon, the following day, in fact. They could not risk waiting any longer. Their previous plan to kill her on the weekend when she would be buying food in the market and thereby be distracted was no longer an option.

"I best get up and get ready, then. We'll kill her this morning," said Aleister.

Dolph and Hans looked at each other and nodded their heads in agreement. Dolph quickly went over to the stove to prepare a quick breakfast. He and Hans were starving. They hadn't eaten for close to twenty-four hours, and they would need their strength and focus for what was to follow in the next few hours.

Dolph, standing at the stove, said, "We need to come up with a viable plan of how to kill her now that we cannot stick with our original idea."

To which Aleister replied, "I've actually been thinking about that for the last few minutes. If she does go into the forest every day, which I'd bet my life she does, I think we should strike her away from town, just as it's getting light as she's crossing the field between the town and forest, where no one will likely see it. Even if she senses me, I doubt she'll tuck tail and run, so we're going to have to face her head-on, unfortunately. Like you said before, Hans, I'm sure she'll be hunting me down at that point. I'm going to ask you two to do something that might endanger your lives, but I think it will work. I want you two waiting at the edge of the forest, so she can see you as she leaves town and enters the field. It is likely she will sense me long before then, so my hope is that when she sees you two standing there, she'll assume one of you is the gifted one. If all goes according to plan, she'll then head straight for you two. I'll be waiting on the edge of town, hidden between the houses. My hope is that she'll be so focused on you two, she won't take her eyes off you, which will give me the advantage to sneak up behind her."

"What if she senses you coming up from behind her?" asked Hans.

"I'm certainly not ruling that out. I will be prepared and expecting that to happen. In that case, a fight will ensue. Plan for the worst but hope for the best. If not, then we get lucky once again," replied Aleister.

"Are you prepared to fight her toe-to-toe?" asked Dolph.

"I honestly don't know. I've never had to fight a Hexies head-on like this. I wouldn't count what happened with Klug as going toe-to-toe because it was unexpected and happened too fast. We shall see. If a fight does ensue, I want you two to get the hell outta there, so you don't die needlessly. Someone will need to live to tell Asta what happened."

Hans and Dolph both nodded their heads in agreement. They were both thinking about how much they would enjoy the chance at directly helping to kill a Hexies, instead of having to stand back and watch. Despite their wishful thinking, they knew very well they would die if they squared off against a Hexies alone. There was a slight chance of success, though, if she was busy fighting Aleister.

LXVI

After they finished eating the breakfast Dolph made, they gathered their things and left the apartment early. They needed to be well in position before Fährlich arrived at the edge of town.

As they walked along the cobblestone streets, they were mentally preparing for what was about to happen. Aleister kept replaying the training he'd received from Asta in his mind, focusing on even the smallest of details that might help him. He knew the training he received from her would be the only thing that might keep him alive today.

When they made it to the edge of town, where the empty field met the forest, they all paused for a moment and looked at each other.

Dolph spoke first. "Yesterday she went between those two houses over there, then entered the forest from the left over there. I suggest you hide downwind from where she'll most likely come through, then try coming up directly behind her. Hans and I will be out waiting in plain view, directly in front of where she entered the forest yesterday, so she'll see us as soon as she clears the houses."

"Sounds like a plan. Again, if a fight ensues, please get the hell outta here as quickly as you can and report back to Asta," said Aleister.

Aleister extended his hand to both of them. "If we don't meet again, gentlemen, please carry on the work. I must say, it's been a pleasure getting to know the both of you. My outlook on life has completely changed since I started this journey."

They all shook hands, then Hans and Dolph turned around and started walking over to their designated position at the edge of the forest. Aleister watched them for a minute before he made his way to the spot that Dolph suggested he hide.

Being that the open field was quite large, it took Hans and Dolph some time to get to the edge of the forest, where they would wait for Fährlich. By this time Aleister was already in position and completely out of sight. As Hans and Dolph stood there, anxiously waiting, neither of them spoke. Instead, they kept their eyes fixated on the spot they were sure Fährlich would suddenly appear from.

Aleister was also anxiously waiting in position, crouched down behind a fence. He had a clear view of the field and would be able to see Fährlich as soon as she cleared the houses and entered the field. The only thing that worried him was that she might decide to change routes and would come up behind him instead.

Thirty minutes went by as the sun started to creep over the horizon. They all soaked in the beauty of that morning, knowing this could be their last sunrise, as evil would soon make an appearance.

A few more minutes went by before Hans gently elbowed Dolph in the side. Dolph slowly moved his head away from the eastern sunrise and over slightly to the edge of town. He knew even before he saw her that he would see Fährlich standing there. She was in the exact spot she had come through yesterday. There she stood, not moving a muscle, only glaring at Hans and Dolph, her eyes fixated on them. They knew she had most certainly sensed Aleister by now and was planning her next move, which, of course, involved killing.

Five minutes went by with the three of them just staring at each other, none of them moving an inch. Then, all of a sudden, Fährlich started calmly walking directly toward Hans and Dolph, her eyes fixated on them.

Hans looked straight at Dolph and said in German, "This is it, Dolph, are you ready?"

"Yes, I'm ready as I'll ever be, Hans," Dolph said, also speaking in German. "I've been ready ever since these bitches took my beloved family from me years ago."

When she was a quarter of the way through the field, Aleister suddenly appeared directly behind Fährlich. Hans and Dolph could see he was sneaking his way through the field, trying to get as close to her as possible without being noticed.

They watched as Aleister slowly crept closer and closer, his H-blades already drawn from their sheaths. Right as Aleister was going to strike her from behind, she whirled around and swiped her long, black nails across his face, sending him staggering backwards. He quickly went back into a fighting stance, and they squared off. Both assumed attack positions and crouched like predators ready to strike. It was in that moment that Hans and Dolph completely disregarded what Aleister had told them, and they took off on a dead run directly toward Aleister and Fährlich.

Aleister could see Hans and Dolph coming at them out of the corner of his right eye, and they were coming in fast. He assumed Fährlich knew this as well. As they stood there, squaring off while looking at each other, each one waiting for the other to make the first move, Aleister noticed she had glanced down at his H-blades.

She then spoke to Aleister and said in a calm, almost sweet voice: "*You must be the gifted one. I sensed you an hour ago. Those must be your trackers coming up behind me now. Very clever, gifted one, but I wonder who's going to die first.*"

As she said that, Dolph and Hans were now within a few meters of Fährlich and closing in fast. Aleister could see Dolph had pulled out a very long blade and was carrying it in his right hand. Hans had also picked up something along the way that looked like a bo staff. They both drew their weapons back and were ready to strike Fährlich, but she was too fast and turned to face them before they could make contact. In that split second, she struck both of them with her long, black nails, sending blood spewing from the necks of both.

While all of this was happening, Aleister's instincts had again taken over. He'd closed in very close to Fährlich, within centimeters of her neck, to be exact. Before it could consciously register in his mind, he'd struck her occipital artery with his H-blade, sending blood spewing from the back of her neck. Fährlich then let out the most hideous, blood-curdling scream he'd ever heard before collapsing to the ground in a heap.

Dolph was lying on the ground, rolling around in pain and holding his neck, blood squirting out between his fingers. Hans was fairly close to Dolph but was crouched over as blood spewed out from his neck, like a dam had burst.

Aleister felt a warm, wet sensation running down his body and into the bottom of his boot. He reached up and touched his face and then looked at his hand. He could see he was also bleeding profusely. He reached into his pocket, grabbed a handkerchief, and went over to Hans first, as he appeared to be the one whose injuries were most urgent. It looked like Fährlich had reopened the same wounds he sustained in Copenhagen.

"Shit, mate! She really opened up your old wounds. Here, put this on to stop the bleeding," said Aleister as he handed Hans the handkerchief.

Moving quickly, he rushed over to Dolph. "Dolph, move your hand so I can see how bad it is."

Dolph hesitantly moved his hand, allowing Aleister to inspect his wound.

"You're very lucky, my friend. She barely missed your jugular. I imagine the only thing that saved all of our lives was the fact that there were three of us. Otherwise, I imagine it'd be me lying there dead. Come on, men, we must get up and leave before someone spots her body and us out in this field. We also need to mend our wounds before we bleed out."

They collected and postured themselves as best they could, considering the immense amount of pain each of them was in. Then they started walking back toward the apartment, though their movements would more accurately be described as staggering. They could see they were drenched in blood and hoped they would go unnoticed in the early dawn hour. Again, the last thing they wanted was to meet the authorities and have to explain their current state.

LXVI

As they staggered along the street, Aleister looked at his companions with a slight grin and said, "I thought I told you bastards to get the hell outta there if she turned to attack me."

Dolph looked at Aleister, his own grin wide, and said, "We had a fairly good idea last night of what was going to happen today. We knew you would say that, so we prepared beforehand and hid some weapons out there in the field. Sorry, Aleister, but we knew if she caught you sneaking up behind her all alone, the only way for you to kill her would be for us to distract her long enough for you to slice her artery. We were willing to accept the risk."

They didn't speak any more after that until they were back in the apartment. The trip took them almost three hours. By that time the streets were bustling with people, and they continued praying that no one would approach them, especially the authorities.

Again, luck appeared to be on their side. They made it back to the apartment with no issues, with only a few people staring at them, clearly wondering what in the hell they'd just been through.

When they made it inside the apartment, they all collapsed inside the black circle and immediately passed out. It was a combination of losing too much blood and sheer exhaustion.

It wasn't until five hours had gone by that they all woke up, in immense pain and covered in dried, crusted blood.

Aleister knew he had to mend their wounds, since he had been the least affected. Trackers always carried good first aid kits in their apartments, so he should be able to find the needed supplies. Fortunately for them,

Aleister had learned a thing or two about mending wounds since he started this journey.

With the first aid kit in hand, he set about helping his new friends. Hans's wounds required stitches, which would be a first for Aleister. He tried reminding himself that it was no different than stitching up his own britches, which was something he'd done many times over the years, especially when he traveled alone. He always carried a small sewing kit with him for just such occasions.

Hans groaned in pain as Aleister carefully placed the stitches. He knew Hans must be suffering a great deal. His wounds were very deep, since Fährlich had struck in the same place as Klug had previously, reopening the wounds deeper than ever. Aleister cringed when he realized he could see part of Hans's exposed esophagus. Aleister shook his head in disbelief, realizing how "lucky" they'd been getting—was it luck, or was something helping them? After seeing and being through what Aleister had over the last few months, he wasn't going to rule out any possibilities.

After he finished with Hans, he shifted toward Dolph, shaking him gently when he realized the other man had slipped back into a light sleep. "Dolph, sorry to wake you, mate, but we need to treat your wounds before they get infected. There's no telling what could have been under Fährlich's nails."

Dolph shifted toward the gifted one with a resigned expression. "Yes, of course, Aleister, by all means, please take care of it."

Aleister could see his wounds were deep as well, but they were not as bad as the ones Hans had suffered. If she'd inserted her nails a little bit farther and to the left, though, Dolph would not be with them now. He would be back lying in the field, in a pool of blood, next to Fährlich's body.

After he finished mending Dolph's wounds, Dolph passed out again. Hans was fast asleep as well. Aleister went to the cabinet and grabbed a bottle of whiskey Dolph had stashed. He set the bottle down in the black circle between them, in case they woke up again in pain. They would at least have some sort of temporary relief from the pain.

Aleister had almost forgotten about his own wounds that needed mending. He picked up the bottle of whiskey again and took a long, deep swig, then went into the bathroom. As he looked in the mirror, he could see four long, deep gashes on the right side of his face that stretched from his ear to the bottom of his chin. He knew he would have scars that would never go away, a constant reminder of the evil that exists in the world. He disinfected and bandaged up the wounds, then went back to the black circle. He took another long swig of whiskey, hoping it would help ease his nerves.

It wasn't long before Aleister passed out as well.

He was awoken the following day by someone grabbing him by the shoulder and shaking him.

"Hey, Aleister, how are you feeling?" asked Hans, holding his own neck and wincing in pain.

"I'm okay," Aleister said. "I just have a pounding headache. How are you, my friend?"

"Sore as hell, but really hungry," replied Hans.

Aleister sat up and looked around. "Where's Dolph?" he asked.

"Don't worry, he's just in the bathroom," replied Hans.

"I must thank you, Aleister," Dolph said as he reappeared, "not only for mending our wounds, but for saving our lives yesterday. We certainly wouldn't be here if it wasn't for you and your quick reaction."

Aleister raised his hand to stop him. "My friends, we saved each other. I wouldn't be here if it weren't for the two of you risking your lives like you did. You were right, Dolph, she was very dangerous. Now I'm certain she knew someone would approach her from behind when she spotted you two at the edge of the forest. She was expecting it. I've never seen anyone move as fast as she did when she lashed out and struck us."

"Neither have I," replied Dolph.

"Nor I. If the three of us weren't together like we were, things would've turned out very differently. Either she would've finished opening the doorway before we knew it, or she would've killed the both of you," said Hans.

Aleister and Dolph looked at each other then back at Hans and nodded in agreement, knowing what Hans was saying was the truth.

"Well, gentlemen, where do we go from here? I can't imagine we want to stay in this city much longer. After all, there is a possibility that the authorities could start looking for three men fitting our description," Aleister said.

"Quite right, we don't want to remain here long. Only as long as it takes to recover enough to travel," replied Dolph.

"Where's our next destination?" asked Aleister.

Hans looked at the other two. "I'm instructed to go to Hammerfest and meet up with Asta."

"Alesiter, you and I are going to Warsaw, Poland, to find and kill another Hexies," said Dolph.

Aleister looked intently at Hans. "Why are you going to meet up with Asta?"

"I was actually supposed to leave and go back to Hammerfest after I helped you arrive in Bremen and meet up with Dolph. However, when I found out how dangerous Fährlich was, I realized you would likely need my help, and I postponed my plans. I wasn't going to leave until we had killed her. After us trackers complete certain assignments, we then take turns watching over and helping the good witches. As you already know, Asta is guarding a black pillar, and it's not a matter of *if* a Hexies comes back there to try to open the doorway but a matter of *when*. We rotate trackers as a way to fool any Hexies that may be watching and following the tracker. Everyone gets complacent at some point and makes mistakes, no matter how good they are. By doing this, it helps keep the trackers fresh, and it also throws off the Hexies if they've learned the habits and patterns of a particular tracker."

"How long will you stay with her, might I ask?" asked Aleister.

"Could be months or longer, not sure exactly. Asta is the one who makes that decision. I imagine it depends on me and when she thinks it's time for me to 'refresh,' as we call it," replied Hans.

Aleister started to think about Asta again, remembering how beautiful and kind she was. He wanted to see her again and hoped that someday that he might, would be sooner rather than later. Finally realizing he hadn't acknowledged what Dolph had told him, he asked, "So, whom are we going to meet in Warsaw?"

"I received a telegram from the tracker who is stationed in Warsaw the day before you and Hans arrived, actually. She's a female from Greece.

Her name is Harmonia, and she's expecting us if we succeeded here. I've met her once before. She's a clever little devil, and she's strong. Her parents were killed by a Hexies when she was only six years old. She was raised by her grandfather, who was a captain in the Greek army—that is, until a good witch found her when she was eighteen years old and showed her a way to avenge her parents."

"Have all trackers had family members killed by a Hexies?" asked Aleister.

"Almost always, yes. For several reasons, it's hard to find someone who would believe this sort of thing even exists, and if they might believe, being willing to lay down their lives is rarer still. I know I wouldn't have believed this sort of evil exists if I hadn't seen it firsthand in what they did to my beautiful wife and my sweet children. A tracker has to give every part of his or her being to the cause—there is no giving up and walking away one day because you get tired of it or scared. That's something a tracker would never do, especially when you know the truth and what is out there. You could never comfortably sleep again at night knowing what lurks in the dark. Being a tracker is the only thing that gives you the peace you seek when everything you loved is killed and taken away from you," replied Dolph.

Aleister understood what Dolph meant and again felt sadness and pity for the trackers. He respected these trackers more than any other person he'd ever met in his life. He had been blessed with the luxury of being raised in a safe and wealthy family, and the only hardship they ever encountered was the occasional sickness. Even then, they would have the best doctors in London visit their house and take care of them until they recovered. He couldn't possibly fathom what these trackers had been through.

"We'll rest here for a few days, until we recover enough," said Dolph. "Then we'll depart for Poland by train. At that point, we'll say our until-we-meet-agains, Hans."

They spent the next three days relaxing, enjoying some good German cuisine, a few German beers, and of course, each other's company. When the fourth day came, they knew they were well enough to travel, and it was time to leave before the authorities could possibly come knocking on their door. They packed what they needed and departed for the train station in Bremen that would take Aleister and Dolph to Warsaw, Poland, and Hans to Denmark, where he would embark by ship to Norway.

"Please take care until we meet again, friends," they told each other before they set off their separate ways.

Aleister was deep in thought as the train chugged along the tracks on that long ride to Warsaw, Poland. He thought about Asta and about how long he would be on the road, tracking down and killing Hexies. He thought about his family back in London and how they must be wondering where he was. They were used to him disappearing for months at a time, as he would sometimes suddenly up and leave with no warning then randomly show up back at home. This time was different, though. He knew he might be gone longer than a few months.

It took several days to reach Warsaw, which was good because their bodies needed the rest.

The train pulled into Warsaw on the night of the third day. Dolph and Aleister were anxious to get off the train, so they quickly grabbed their bags. Once they stepped off the train, Dolph stood there for a moment, looking around until he spotted Harmonia standing under one of the train station's signs. Dolph waved to her as they walked over to where she was standing. They greeted each other with a hug, then Dolph introduced Aleister to her. Aleister was a bit taken aback by how good her English was.

"It's a pleasure to meet you, Aleister. I always enjoy meeting a new gifted one. Come, let us go. Stag stew and the black circle await us," said Harmonia.

LXVI

As JD, Jason, Chung, and Crowley sped down that empty desert highway in Crowley's old Chevelle toward the nothingness, he finished telling the story of his father and everything he knew about that time.

"My father, Aleister, spent another fifteen years traveling all over Europe, meeting new trackers and killing Hexies. That is, until every last Hexies in Europe was thought to be dead. However, what Asta had feared most would happen, happened. A small group of Hexies left Europe without anyone's knowledge and made it to America. We now know they settled in Bangor, Maine. No one knew for sure when they left Europe or where they settled. We only knew that a small group of Hexies had escaped to America. I've spent most of my life looking for their descendants, fearing that they'd created a black pillar somewhere in America, and once I saw the news report, I knew my worst fears had come true."

There were a lot of questions running through JD's mind as he sat in the Chevelle's bucket seat next to Crowley, but there was one question he just had to ask.

"What happened to your father after he quit tracking and killing Hexies?" asked JD.

"I thought you might ask," Crowley said, glancing at him. "After my father went back to London, he continued the training Asta had started him on. He also continued studying witchcraft and dark evil, so that he would never lose his edge. He never stopped, until his death in 1947. A year after my father went back to London, my mother showed up on his doorstep one day and gave him quite a surprise. My parents, Aleister and Asta, were married not long after, and five years later, I was born."

"I knew it! I had a feeling by the way you said Aleister felt and talked about Asta. So that would make you about sixty-five years old, right?" asked JD.

"Yes, it would. I'm no spring chicken, boy."

"I take it you're a gifted one as well, having a good witch as your mother and Aleister as your father?" asked JD.

"Yes, and maybe a little bit more," Crowley replied with a slight grin. "I, of course, was trained basically from birth and have been preparing for this very thing my whole life."

"Now I have to ask, where the hell do we go from here?" asked JD.

"Our plan now is to go see a good witch who lives in the Sonoran Desert of Arizona. We will need her help and guidance with this if we want any chance at succeeding. She's a very old but powerful witch who knew my mother. There are now two black pillars in America that have opened the doorway to dark evil, that we know of anyway. This is obviously a method to allow more dark evil to enter our world, which means twice the carnage at twice the speed will now occur. I'm wondering if, when the one in Maine was triggered and opened by your friend Matt, the one in Utah opened as well. I'm betting that was the plan all along, set up by the Hexies that created them," replied Crowley.

Jason and Chung stayed silent as they raced along toward Arizona. Obviously deep in thought, they were still trying to process the story that Crowley had just told them. Their world had just been turned upside down.

JD sat there trying to process it all as well. To him, what was happening was almost like being in a dream, a nightmare to be exact. None of it seemed to be real, and he was hoping to wake up at any minute.

"Judging from the map I checked earlier, we have about a nine-hour drive," said Crowley.

What they'd just witnessed at the Verwer farm had shaken the boys up so badly that they wanted the drive to last forever, so they wouldn't have to face what lay ahead. They just wanted this nightmare to end, for good. Mostly, they wanted things to go back to the way they were before, so they could return home, see their families again, and, though it shocked them to realize it, go back to school.

As they made their way to the desolate Sonoran Desert, they only stopped for food and gas. When they did stop at gas stations, they could see people were really starting to panic about what was happening out east and the fact it seemed to be spreading. They could hear people whispering crazy things and talking about the end of the world.

When they finally arrived at the edge of the Sonoran Desert, they saw a strange old wooden sign on the right-hand side of the road that had a black circle with a painting of a ram's skull in the middle of it. Crowley suddenly turned the car hard right and continued speeding down a dirt road that was a few feet in front of the sign.

JD recognized the black circle and skull and knew they were on the road that would lead them to the old witch. He could see Crowley was deep in thought as they drove, and it felt wrong to bother him with questions, so JD sat there in silence as well.

They drove south for several hours down that dirt road, heading deeper and deeper into the Sonoran Desert. They would occasionally see a jack rabbit run across the road or a bird swoop down in front of the headlights of the Chevelle. The boys knew they were in the middle of nowhere with no one to help them if something went wrong, and they couldn't help feeling uneasy.

JD guessed they'd been driving on the little road for two or three hours when it finally turned left around a small mountain. As they rounded the mountain, he could see a small light shining in the middle of the nothingness.

"See that light, boys? That's where the old witch lives. Now, one thing to keep in mind, she's very old and is sometimes crass, so don't be alarmed with her bluntness. As she puts it, she's too old to give a shit about people's feelings," said Crowley.

Hearing that made JD curious and anxious to see who this old witch was.

As they got close, they could make out a small shack that was sitting next to a small flowing stream. They could see the moon's light shining off the stream. This was a first time for JD and his friends to be in a desert like this. They were in awe of how magical and how empty it seemed, all at the same time.

As they pulled up to the shack, parked the car, and turned the engine off, Crowley rolled down his window and yelled, "Harmonia, it's me, Crowley! Don't come out shooting!"

The door to the shack started creaking open ever so slowly, then stopped about halfway. A woman's voice said, "How the hell are ya, you old bastard? I've been wondering when your tall, skinny ass would show up at my door again." The door then opened all the way, and out she came.

When she stepped outside and JD saw her, he immediately thought she wasn't bad-looking for an older woman. She was thin, with long silver hair that went all the way down to her knees. She looked tough, and her skin looked like old worn, shiny leather. To the boys, she looked like she could kick some ass at the drop of a hat, and this made JD grin. The boys could also see she was cradling a long, double-barreled shotgun in her arms.

"I know why you're here. It's begun, hasn't it? The day we've feared for so many years is finally here," said Harmonia.

Crowley opened the driver's side door and stepped out of the car. Walking over to her, he pulled her into his arms and gave her a long hug. "Unfortunately, yes, Harmonia, it's begun, and it's spreading as we speak. It's good to see you again, old friend, even under these circumstances. Every time I leave this place, I never know if I'll return."

Harmonia looked over at the car and, with a slight grin, asked, "Who the hell are these little shits with you?"

Aleister let out a loud chuckle and replied, "These boys saw the Malum and survived. Their friend touched the black pillar and opened the doorway, and, of course, he didn't survive, but these boys managed to get away. The black pillar was in a cemetery in Bangor, Maine, all this time, and we found another one in Utah, along with the descendants of the Verwer family, so there's two that we know of. One more thing, we saw The Malum, or should I say its black claws, at the Verwer farm. We were damn lucky it was daytime or we would not be here now. The boy in the front seat is a gifted one and probably the reason they're still alive after seeing it in the flesh in Maine. Since their other friend actually touched the pillar and released it, unfortunately, there was no saving him."

Hearing Crowley say he was a gifted one sent shivers up JD's spine. It hit him in that moment the reason why Crowley had found him in the library that day, just out of the blue the way he did. Coming out of nowhere like a creepy ghost.

"Get your little asses outta the car and let's have a look at you," said Harmonia.

The three of them slowly stepped out of the car and walked over to where Crowley and Harmonia were standing. They were sure to keep somewhat of a distance between them, as they still weren't sure what to make of Harmonia. As they were walking over, JD noticed there was a large black circle that looked like it encompassed the whole shack. He instantly knew what it was and figured there had to be a black ram's skull on top of her shack. *She's protecting herself,* he thought. It then hit JD who Harmonia must be, and he looked over at Crowley. "Is this the Harmonia from the story, the one from Greece you told us about?"

Before Aleister could respond, Harmonia said, "You're damn right that's me! Came here from Europe after Aleister and me killed off all those goddamn forsaken Hexies. Some slipped through the cracks, though, and Crowley and I have been hunting their descendants ever since. We were obviously too late."

"I thought you were just a tracker, though? Crowley never mentioned you were a good witch as well." JD hoped he hadn't offended her, but the question had slipped out before he had a chance to consider that it might sound rude.

Harmonia let out a loud, boisterous laugh and said, "That's just like ole Crowley to leave out important details when he tells a story. I could tell you things, son, that Aleister, Asta, and me saw when we were hunting Hexies that would make you cry like a baby. I best not, though, because we're going to need you boys to be brave and confident through this shitstorm, or we're all gonna die."

JD loved the way she talked, and he could hear she had an accent when she spoke. Her accent was beautiful, like music to his ears. He could tell

Jason and Chung liked her as well by the smirks on their faces as she talked. They'd never met anyone like her in their lives, and it made them forget for a moment the horrific things that were happening back in their hometown.

"Well, hell, men, let's not stand out here all night and freeze our skinny asses off. It gets damn cold in the desert during this time of year. Let's go inside, and I'll put a pot of coffee on and warm your little bellies right up," said Harmonia.

LXVI

As they walked inside the shack, JD noticed it was unlike anything he'd ever seen before. There were all kinds of interesting things throughout the little structure, things he had no clue about—trinkets, small statues, carvings, and just overall strange things. The shack was also much bigger than he originally thought, as it stretched quite a ways out from the back. He couldn't see its true size from the front since it was dark outside.

Harmonia walked them over to a long wooden table that had two long bench seats and said, "Sit down, and I'll put the kettle on. Who takes sugar and cream with their coffee? I also have black tea if that tickles your fancy."

Everyone raised their arms except Crowley. "I'll have black tea, Harmonia," Crowley told her.

"I knew you'd say that, Aleister. Ya haven't changed much since you were just a little turd, but I like that. It's good to have some constants in this godforsaken world."

"Wait a minute, did you just call him Aleister?" asked Jason.

"Yes, of course I did, son, because that's his name. He's Aleister Crowley the II. I know he likes to be called Crowley to avoid stupid questions from people who know about his famous father, but I call him what I want," replied Harmonia.

Crowley was smiling slightly as she said that. Everyone was then silent as Harmonia finished making their coffee and Crowley's black tea. After she finished brewing their drinks, she carried them over on a wooden plate and set them down on the table. Everyone grabbed theirs and began to take small sips, as they were still very hot.

Harmonia walked over a few feet and sat down in an old wooden rocking chair. Soon, she had started to rock back and forth.

"Crowley, there's something I've been wanting to tell you for some time. I didn't think it was important until you told me these boys' friend touched the black pillar and released the Malum. Your mother once told me of a theory she had about when a black pillar is created. She said they're created from the energy of the Hexies that creates it, which means it's tied to the two Hexies that created it. Which may also mean that when a Hexies is killed, the black pillar may die with it because the energy source dies when the Hexies dies. She believed their energy is needed to sustain it and keep it alive. Your mother told me this because the pillars she and the other good witches guarded for so many years not once ever had a Hexies try to approach them to release the Malum. None of us knew this beforehand, of course, so we played the card of better to be safe than sorry and guarded them. After we killed all the Hexies in Europe and before she went to England to be with your father, she sat down and told me all of this," said Harmonia.

"If this were true, then why was the black pillar in Bangor, Maine, still alive, even though the Hexies that created it died over one hundred years ago?" asked Crowley.

"Yes, I've been wondering that myself ever since you first mentioned it. The only conclusion I can come up with is that somehow the descendants—the bloodline of the Verwer Hexies that created it—were keeping it alive all these years. They've been waiting all this time for someone to go into that cemetery, touch the black pillar, and open the doorway. This is all theory, of course, but it makes the most sense."

"What should be our next plan of attack?" asked Crowley.

"I knew you'd ask that next. We must kill the Verwer descendants, of course, and completely wipe out their bloodline. Keep in mind the Verwers you encountered in Utah are Hexies. Why in the hell they didn't try to kill you all baffles me beyond belief. There must've been something a helluva lot more important, and whatever that reason is may prove to be more dangerous than they are. One other thing that's been bothering me as well is being there were multiple Hexies in Maine and at the Verwer farm, I'm not sure why they didn't open the doorway themselves years ago when they created the pillars, since we always thought it only takes two Hexies to open the doorway. Well, in our defense, we witches always knew we didn't have an exact answer for everything, so some things we thought to be true may not have been.

"The other serious problem we're facing is that the Malum has already been released into our world. Just simply wiping out their bloodline along with the black pillars may not actually stop the Malum at this point. It may only close the doorway."

"What do we do, then?" asked Crowley.

"Before your dear mother departed this earth, Aleister, she left me all of her journals and all of the information she had gathered over the years pertaining to Hexies and dark evil. It may take me days to go through all of it, but she may have unknowingly left us the answer we're looking for. If not, everyone will die."

That was something JD and his friends did not want to hear. Instantly, they felt themselves freeze in place and their hearts drop.

Crowley looked over at the boys and said, "I know that's not what you wanted to hear, boys. I told you she'd be blunt, which is better than lying to you. Our focus now needs to be killing all of the Verwer descendants while Harmonia looks for an answer to our other problem."

Crowley looked directly at JD and said, "JD, I'm sure you heard me tell Harmonia you're a gifted one. Yes, it's true, and yes, that is how I found you in the library that day. Being that my mother was a good witch, I also inherited her witch senses."

Crowley then reached behind his back to grab something. The boys watched intently as Crowley drew out what looked like a knife. He set it down on the table so the boys could see it clearly. What they saw was the coolest-looking knife that any of them had ever seen. It had a shiny black wooden handle but was textured in certain spots so as not to slip from the hand. The shape of the blade was unlike anything they'd ever seen before.

"Boys, this here is an H-blade. It was my father's, and it has killed many Hexies. JD, you're about to get a crash course in how to use an H-blade. We don't have a lot of time, so I'll teach you the most important aspects that will hopefully keep you alive, and maybe even successful," said Crowley.

Crowley looked over at Harmonia and asked, "I'm assuming you still have the other H-blades I left here years ago?"

"What's the expression Americans use? Does a bear shit in the woods? I've always liked that one. Of course I do, my dear Aleister," replied Harmonia.

Harmonia walked over to a cabinet on the wall that had a carving of a dragon on it. She opened it up and retrieved something rectangular that was wrapped in a black cloth, then walked over to Crowley and handed it to him. Crowley set it down on the table and pulled aside the black cloth to reveal an old wooden box. He opened the wooden box, and the boys could see two H-blades sitting inside. The handles on these looked slightly different than Crowley's. These H-blades had dark brown handles that looked like they were made from the wood of a walnut tree. They knew this because of their high-school woodworking class.

JD looked over at Harmonia, who had sat back down in her rocking chair, and asked, "What's the dragon carving on your cabinet?"

"That, son, is the Greek dragon Pytho. In Greek mythology, he was thought to inhabit the city of Delphi, where I was born and raised. He was considered to be one of the biggest and most fearsome dragons in Greek mythology. He was also Apollo's biggest enemy, who was thought to inhabit the city of Delphi. That's a good story for another time, but right now, we need to come up with a plan of how you guys will go about killing the Verwer bloodline."

"That's been running through my head ever since we left the farm. I knew one way or another we'd have to end up killing them. Once I started driving down the dirt road that led to their farm, I could sense they were Hexies," said Crowley.

The three of us all looked at Crowley, and Chung asked, "What do you want us to do, Crowley?"

"Glad you asked, boy, because I will need your help. The Verwer family has been playing off like they're ignorant hillbillies, but they are far from that. They are smart, calculating, and above all, extremely dangerous. There's no telling how many there are out there at that farm, which brings me to my next point. I'm going to need you two, Chung and Jason, to do some reconnaissance on their farm, to see exactly how many Hexies there are out there. If there are too many, then our strategy will need to be vastly different than what I'm thinking. If JD and I get too close to their farm again, they'll sense us, and I doubt we'll all survive next time if we're unprepared. I have equipment that will aid you when we attack, such as optics, night vision, and guns. Guns are only to be used when I say so, or if your lives absolutely depend on it. Firing a gun at a Hexies will only stop them momentarily, then you run like hell. Keep that in mind. If there are more than one, forget about it, because you're dead. Hexies need to be sliced through the occipital artery with an H-blade to be fully killed, like you heard in the story I told," replied Crowley.

"Damn, I wish I was young enough to help you. I would love to help kill those sons of bitches!" said Harmonia.

Crowley let out a chuckle and said, "I wish too, Harmonia! You were the best tracker for many years, but now you have a much more important task: finding an answer that will save the human race. I would appreciate it if you gave Jason and Chung some tips and tactics on how to do reconnaissance, as I imagine they've never done it before. This mission is going to be filled with many first times, which may actually prove to help us. I'm not sure why I feel that, but it's a feeling I have."

"Certainly, Aleister! I'd be more than happy to. Anything that helps kill those bloody Hexies," replied Harmonia with her face twisted into a fierce scowl.

"Thank you, Harmonia. I'm assuming you still have the proper training equipment out back behind your shack?" asked Aleister.

"Of course, and now there's a fire pit in the back, with a stack of wood so you can train by firelight," replied Harmonia.

"Good! Come, boy, let's get started. Every minute we waste makes our enemy stronger," said Crowley.

LXVI

Crowley spent the next six hours giving JD a crash course in H-blades and killing Hexies. Meanwhile, Harmonia talked to Jason and Chung about reconnaissance and the best way to avoid getting ripped apart by a Hexies. Around 5:00 a.m., JD finally collapsed from exhaustion. Crowley lifted him up and put him down on one of the cots Harmonia had prepared for the boys. He let the boys sleep until noon, knowing the consequences would be grave if they weren't fully rested and focused for what they were about to face.

Once he felt they would be rested enough, Crowley came into their makeshift room and woke the three of them. "Boys, get up. We have a lot to prepare today before we leave early tomorrow morning. Harmonia has also prepared you some food, so go eat first, then meet me out front by the car."

The boys were still half asleep as they slowly rolled off their cots, put on their shoes, and went into the kitchen. After eating a quick meal of bread, eggs, coffee, and coues deer sausage they went out front, where Crowley was sitting in a chair behind a tripod that had a spotting scope mounted to it.

"Come over here, boys. I want to introduce you to a friend of mine. This is a 40X60 Leupold spotting scope. It will allow you two, Jason and Chung, to observe the Verwer farm from quite a distance without them seeing you, hopefully. Understand, all we need to know is exactly how many Hexies are living on the farm, and you may need to observe for quite some time to make sure you've counted all of them. I'm sure Harmonia told you last night that anytime there are two or more of you, one person must be the lookout and always be on alert. You can't lose focus for a single second while the spotter is on the scope. It could spell death if you do. Hexies are smart and extremely fast. The spotter must be focused at all times as well, because you may only get a flash of a person as they walk past a window or an open door. Getting an exact count of how many Hexies there are is crucial to our success, and possibly our very survival. Never before has anyone faced this many Hexies at once, so this will be a challenge. When we were at the farm, I observed a mesa about a half mile south of the Verwer farm. That's where you'll spot from."

"What the heck is a mesa?" asked Jason.

"I forgot you boys wouldn't know that, being from the East. It's a flat, isolated hill or mountain in the desert, like a plateau. Mesas are all over the desert. You'll have a good vantage point from on top, but you'll need to belly crawl before you get to the edge of the mesa. Plan on belly crawling at least a hundred yards before coming to the edge, otherwise they'll easily spot you on the skyline. Once you're on the edge you'll need to stay down the entire time. If you can see them from the top of the mesa when you're standing up, then they can see you. Remember that. If you're spotted, it's game over."

Chung and Jason glanced at each other with worried looks but still nodded their heads that they understood.

JD looked at Crowley and asked, "Why not just give them the bag of black sand and the painting of the ram's skull so they can make the circle that will protect them?"

"You mean the BWC?" replied Crowley. The boys all had confused looks on their faces. "It stands for Black Witches Circle, at least that's what we call it. Unfortunately, a BWC only works if there's a good witch or gifted one inside of it. Trust me, nothing would make me feel more at ease than Jason and Chung being protected by one, but it is not an option in this case."

"Oh, I see," said JD.

"Rest up and eat a lot today, boys, because we leave early tomorrow morning. Jason and Chung, I want you guys on this spotting scope all day today, practicing and getting familiar with it. It will take some time for your eyes to adjust to looking through it for long periods of time. Try to find the small deer that inhabit this desert—they're called coues deer. They're nicknamed the gray ghost because they're extremely hard to spot, and once you do spot them, they have a tendency to up and vanish right before your eyes. You've actually been eating coues meat since you arrived here. JD, you come with me. We have more to discuss about killing Hexies, and also how to make sure you don't get killed by a Hexies."

Jason and Chung immediately sat down behind the spotting scope and took turns glassing the desert landscape, looking for the gray ghosts, while Crowley and JD walked back into Harmonia's shack and discussed strategies and tactics.

Crowley talked to JD for several hours about everything while JD sat intently listening to every word Crowley said, knowing his very survival might hinge on something Crowley told him during their impromptu training sessions.

Around 8:00 p.m., after it had gotten dark, Harmonia, who had been gone for most of the day, came back from wherever she had been and yelled, "Dinner is ready, men. Come and get it!"

They all met at the kitchen table, looking at each other as they sat down. There was a lot going through their minds. No one said it, but they all knew this might be one of the last meals they would be able to have with each other, and the possibility that it could be their last day on Earth was on the mind of each of them.

After they finished their meal, Crowley spoke up and said, "Go get some sleep, boys. We leave at 6:00 a.m."

They all stood up from the kitchen table without saying a word, walked to the room where their cots were, and stretched out across them. Each of them quickly fell asleep.

Around 5:45 a.m., the boys were awakened to Crowley's booming voice. "Up and at 'em, boys! We need to eat a quick breakfast before we take off. You'll need your stomachs full. Harmonia packed each of you some food and plenty of water, especially you two, as you'll be on the mesa for a while today." Crowley looked at Jason and Chung.

The boys again stumbled out of bed, half awake. They all needed more sleep after everything they'd been through over the last week. They felt like they were in a drunken stupor as they struggled to put their clothes on.

Crowley walked off into the kitchen as the boys finished getting ready.

When the three of them joined the adults, they were greeted by Harmonia, who blurted out in her loud Greek accent, "Morning, men! I've prepared something special for you little heathens—pancakes with venison breakfast sausage and some strong coffee that'll knock your pants off."

JD thought to himself that he was going to miss hearing Harmonia's beautiful accent and her funny comments. If he actually survived this ordeal, he would love to come back and visit Harmonia again, so he could listen to her tell stories about her life. He could only imagine the crazy things she'd seen and done during her lifetime.

After Crowley finished eating, he stood up from the table and went over to give Harmonia a long hug. "Until we meet again, Harmonia. It's always a pleasure. Thank you again, for everything."

"Of course, Aleister, my dear. You know it is my pleasure. You're like a son to me. Once you kill those dirty bastards, you'd better damn well come back here. I'll do my best to find an answer in your mother's journal about getting rid of the Malum."

"There's no place I'd rather be than here," said Crowley with a chuckle.

Looking over at the boys, he said, "Mount up, boys. It's time." Giving them each a stern look, he headed outside and climbed inside his Chevelle.

The boys finished their last bites of food and coffee before they stood up and thanked Harmonia for everything she had done for them. With a collective resigned sigh, they took their places inside the Chevelle.

Before Crowley fired up the engine, he turned back, looking at the boys. "Double-check you have everything, especially you, JD. Without your H-blades you're as useless as tits on a boar against a Hexies."

The boys checked to make sure they had everything then nodded at Crowley, letting him know they were ready. Crowley turned back in his seat and fired up the Chevelle's horses, then backed the car up and turned it north toward Utah. He laid a patch as he sped off through the dusty desert road. Jason and Chung were staring out the back window and noticed Harmonia was standing just outside her front door, watching them as they left. They looked at each other, and neither had a doubt about what the other one was thinking. They'd much rather stay with Harmonia, since they knew where they were headed was hell and pure dread.

LXVI

No one spoke for a while as they drove along that dusty desert road. Finally, Crowley said, "Boys, let's go over the plan again, in detail. Hexies don't leave much room for error; making a mistake with a Hexies will most likely be the last you ever make."

They spent the next several hours as they drove toward Utah going over the plan and discussing possible scenarios to better prepare themselves for the unpredictable. They only stopped once, for lunch and gas.

They made it to the edge of Orangeville, Utah, about nine hours later. The time was 3:30 p.m.

When they were a few miles from the Verwer farm, Crowley pulled the Chevelle over to the side of the road, looked back at Jason and Chung, and said, "The mesa you'll be spotting from is the one that's a few miles in front of us. I won't go any closer right now for fear they'll sense us. JD and I will wait in the car, just to be safe. What I want you boys to do is hike to the top of the mesa, so we can see how long it takes. You'll need to figure out the best route to get to the top of the mesa, but I don't want you going to the edge to do any spotting today. Tomorrow morning we'll wake up early so you can go spotting, but today we just need to know how long it takes you to hike to the top. Mesas are full of cliffs and loose rocks, and, of course, since this is the first time either of you have hiked a steep mesa, you should be extremely cautious."

Crowley told the boys good luck and looked at his watch so he could time their progress. Jason and Chung grabbed the water and food Harmonia had prepared for them and set off on their assignment. Crowley and JD then sat mostly in silence as they waited for Jason and Chung to return.

Four hours had gone by when they finally saw Jason and Chung coming into view as they walked back toward the car.

"Right at four hours—that's about how long I figured it would take them," Crowley said, seeming pleased. "They look beat down, and rightly so. They probably hiked about twelve miles."

When they made it back to the Chevelle and climbed into the back seat, Crowley turned back to them and said, "Glad to see you boys made it back. Any problems?"

"None at all. Just ran into some snakes, lizards, and a few rabbits along the way," replied Chung.

"Yeah, we did exactly as you instructed. We went as far as we could without going to the edge of the mesa and found the best route to take tomorrow," said Jason.

"Good boys. You'll start hiking at first light tomorrow. We'll go to another town tonight to sleep and eat. We want to keep our distance from the farm," said Crowley.

He fired up the Chevelle, flipped a u-turn, and started heading southeast, toward a town they'd passed on the way called Castle Dale. Once they arrived in Castle Dale, Crowley parked in front of a café called The Sunglow, which also had a motel attached to the back of it.

"This looks like a decent place. We'll eat here and spend the night. The sign says the café opens up at 6:00 a.m., so we'll wake up then, eat, then drive back to the exact spot we went today," said Crowley, glancing around at the three boys.

They all climbed out of the Chevelle and went inside the café. There were several people already seated inside who looked to be local farmers. They were greeted with a nod and, "Good evening, Gentlemen" from one of the farmers who was already seated and eating.

The waitress flashed a friendly smile and said, "Please sit anywhere, and I'll be with you in just a moment."

They looked for a booth that was the farthest away from anyone, so no one could hear what they were going to discuss.

Once they were settled, JD was the first one to speak. "Believe it or not, I'm going to miss these small-town cafés."

"Me too. I've grown to love the atmosphere of these small, out-of-the-way towns," Jason agreed.

Within a few minutes the waitress came over, took their orders, and asked where they were from. Crowley took over, telling her, "We're actually from the East, Vermont to be exact." Hearing Crowley say that, the boys knew it was in their best interest not to say exactly where they were from.

The waitress then said in a slightly Southern drawl, "Do ya'll know what's going on back there in the East? Crazy things are happening, and people are panicking. Some are even saying it's the end of the world, and it's spreading. At least, that's what I've been seeing on TV."

They all looked at each other, and Crowley replied, "Yes, ma'am, we're aware of it, and unfortunately, it is getting worse. People should be panicking." The waitress looked a bit taken aback by Crowley's remark. She didn't say anything, though—she just turned around and walked back into the kitchen.

"I probably shouldn't have said that last remark, but it just kind of came out," said Crowley with a shake of his head.

"Well, it's the truth, and people have a right to know. Unfortunately, most people wouldn't believe us anyway," said Chung.

They all sat in silence until their food arrived. They were starving at this point, and they spent the next ten minutes devouring their burgers and fries with nary a word spoken between them.

After they finished eating, they went up to the cashier, paid for their food, and reserved a room for the night.

As they walked outside to grab their things, Crowley said, "It's almost 10:00, boys. I say we get some sleep. We have a big day tomorrow. If we get an exact count of how many Hexies are at the Verwer farm tomorrow, then JD and I will be going in the following day. Dark evil grows stronger with each passing day."

When JD heard Crowley say that, he instantly got a huge lump in his throat and couldn't swallow. He knew that day was coming, and he'd been dreading it, but now it was becoming a reality.

They grabbed their things from the Chevelle and made their way to room 107, where they would be staying the night. Once they were inside, they all crashed within minutes, especially Chung and Jason. Hiking twelve miles in the span of a few hours was more than they'd ever done before, and they were exhausted.

LXVI

It seemed like they had just fallen asleep when they were
awakened by Crowley's booming voice: "Wake up, boys! It's six bells on
the dot!"

The thunderous words jolted the boys out of bed, scaring the hell out of
them.

"Judas Priest, Crowley! You scared the shit out of me. A slight nudge or
whisper in my ear would do just fine," JD said grumpily.

Crowley's response was just a slight mischievous grin.

The boys stumbled out of bed and pulled on some clothes before they
made their way to the café for breakfast. They all ordered pancakes,
bacon, and eggs for breakfast and tried to make light of the dire situation
they were facing by recounting humorous stories of their
youth—anything to take their minds off of what was about to come.

After breakfast they went back to their room, grabbed their things, then
piled into the ole black Chevelle. Crowley sat for several moments lost in
thought before inserting the key into the ignition and firing up the engine.
JD, who was riding shotgun, could only imagine what was going through
the man's head. He hoped they were positive thoughts or strategies rather
than dread and despair. Crowley was a tough cookie to read, though. The
most emotion he'd ever really shown them was when he was with
Harmonia. She seemed to bring out a happy side of him that otherwise
stayed buried.

As they sped down the old asphalt highway toward the mesa, no one said
a word, and rightly so. Knowing he might be facing death would leave a

man to his thoughts and make him contemplate his life. The boys now understood how a man staring death in the face felt, and it wasn't a good feeling. However, this was nothing new to Crowley, as he'd been preparing for this type of situation most of his life, and he had faced death several times before and survived.

It wasn't long before the mesa came into view, and the boys knew there was no turning back now. Crowley pulled the Chevelle over to the exact spot they had stopped the day before and turned off the engine.

He turned around to talk to Jason and Chung, making eye contact with each of them, his face serious. "It is time, boys. Remember everything we've discussed, as your life depends on it. Above all else, do not get spotted on the skyline of the mesa. Once you're a hundred yards from the edge, you must get down and belly crawl to the edge before setting up the spotting scope. Again, whoever is not on the spotting scope must be alert at all times. I can't emphasize that enough. The Verwer farm is only a half mile from the mesa, and we have no idea if they can gain easy access to the top from there, but you need to play it as if they can. They've lived their whole lives in that place, so they know the area better than anyone else, which gives them an advantage. Your best defense against these Hexies is to not get spotted, and your second-best defense, and only defense if they spot you, is to simply run as fast as you can. If you're approached by anyone, and I mean anyone, I don't care if it's a little kid, a beautiful girl, or a kind-looking motherly type, you run like hell back here without stopping for so much as a second. Hexies can be anyone, and you'll never know because you'll be dead in an instant if they get within killing range of you. They're going to be on high alert now, since they know we know who they are."

Jason and Chung nodded their heads in agreement and climbed out of the car. Crowley got out and popped the trunk so they could get the spotting scope and their supplies, in case they had to spend some lengthy time on the mesa, which was likely. The time was 7:45 a.m. when they left.

Crowley got back into the car, and they both watched them as they walked out of sight.

"How concerned are you they'll run into trouble?" asked JD.

Crowley turned and locked all the car's doors, then looked over at JD with a straight face, showing no emotion. "Truthfully, I'm not sure, JD. I've never encountered this many Hexies together in one spot. The old saying of strength in numbers applies tenfold when it comes to Hexies. One Hexies alone is dangerous enough and will literally rip your body apart if given the chance, but multiple Hexies is unheard of and undocumented. I sat down with Harmonia while we were at her place, and she documented everything we've seen so far, in case future generations need to know what happened here. The only chance we have is finding out exactly how many Hexies there are before we attack. We must keep a precise count of how many we kill as we're killing them, to be sure we will not be surprised. Being caught off guard by even one Hexies we're unaware of might spell death for us both."

It wasn't quite the answer JD was hoping for. He couldn't blame Crowley, though, for not knowing if his friends would be all right, because it was uncharted territory for him as well.

It wasn't long before JD drifted off to sleep and was awakened by Crowley opening the driver's side door and getting out.

"Is everything all right?" asked JD.

"Everything's fine. It's about noon, and I'm hungry. I'm getting some food and water from the trunk. Would you like something?" replied Crowley.

"Hell yes! My belly button's rubbing a blister on my backbone," said JD with a smirk.

Crowley let out a slight chuckle as he was grabbing food and water from the back. It made JD smile hearing Crowley laugh because he was used to him always being so serious.

When Crowley came and sat back down in the driver's seat, he noticed Crowley again locking all the car's doors. Seeing this reminded JD of the seriousness of their situation. To JD, it seemed Crowley didn't fear anything, but Crowley was slightly worried, and he wasn't taking any chances.

He handed JD a sandwich he'd bought from a local gas station, some Twinkies, and an empty plastic soda bottle that had been filled with water at the motel. They made small talk about their personal lives as they sat and ate and drank.

After they finished, Crowley said, "JD, by all means, get some more sleep. Being rested will make you alert and frosty."

Hearing Crowley say that, it didn't take long for JD to drift back into a deep slumber. A few hours went by, and JD slowly started to wake up.

Crowley looked over at him. "They've been out there for seven hours now. We'll wait here as long as it takes, but if they don't come back by tomorrow morning, we'll have to make up a new plan and assume something terrible happened. If they don't get off that mesa before it gets dark, it would be best for them to just stay up there. Hiking around a mesa full of cliffs and large boulders in the dark can be deadly, even with a flashlight."

A few more hours went by, and JD noticed the sun was starting to set, which meant it was past 6:00 p.m. He wasn't too worried about his friends yet, but he was on the verge of it. The way he figured, they had an hour, tops, to show back up.

LXVI

Several more hours went by, and the sun continued to sink farther in the sky. It was pitch-black outside, and JD was officially worried. The silence and eeriness grated at his nerves, leaving him covered in goosebumps. As he sat there, wondering what was going on in Crowley's head, someone all of a sudden started pounding on the passenger side window. JD almost jumped out of his seat and over into Crowley's lap. JD hadn't noticed, but in that split second, Crowley had already retrieved his H-blade from behind his back and was in a semi-ready attack position. That is, until he noticed it was Chung and Jason who were pounding on the window.

"Hurry, boy! Open the door and let them in," said Crowley.

JD quickly unlocked and opened the door, and Jason and Chung piled in as fast as they could.

They were both completely out of breath, and it appeared they'd been running as fast as they could. JD could see they looked very frightened, their faces as white as ghosts.

Crowley immediately fired up the Chevelle's engine, flipped a u-turn like the previous day, and sped off. JD knew Crowley wasn't going to stick around and take any chances.

"Catch your breath, boys, then tell us everything you saw. No detail is too small," said Crowley as he sped down that dark, empty road toward Castle Dale.

A few minutes went by with nothing but the sounds of Jason and Chung struggling to even their breathing. Finally, Jason said in a wavering tone, "There are seven of them—we counted seven Hexies. We also saw a black pillar between the house and barn. They were in a circle and were praying to it for hours and—"

Chung, visibly shaking, cut Jason off mid-sentence, blurting out: "We saw it!"

"Come again? You saw what?" asked Crowley.

"The evil . . . the . . . the Malum. We saw it. It was the same thing that killed our friend Matthew. Once we saw it, we left as fast as we could," said Chung as he fought back the tears that were crowding his eyes.

"So it is definitely here now. It won't be long before it starts consuming everyone around here and spreading, if it hasn't already," said Crowley. He then looked over at JD and said, "We must strike first thing tomorrow, at first light. If they have moved the black pillar from inside the barn to outside, that gives us an advantage. There's no way they could've created another pillar that fast—at least, we'd better hope not, because if they have, we won't last long."

"Why would they move the black pillar outside? There's a huge risk we might see it, right?" asked JD.

"Arrogance," replied Crowley.

A few minutes went by, then Crowley asked, "Are you sure there are only seven of them? You must be absolutely certain of that, or JD and I will be walking into a death trap tomorrow when we roll into the farm."

Chung and Jason almost spoke in unison, each of them saying vehemently, "Yes, we're sure."

Crowley nodded his head, hoping they knew what they were saying. He knew he had no choice but to trust their judgment either way. "I want to hear everything you saw from the beginning to the end. Chung, I want you to start first. Tell your story in detail, then I want to hear your take after that, Jason. Each person observes things differently, so one will catch something the other doesn't."

JD had always respected Crowley, but now he was really starting to see how sharp he truly was. Watching the older man take control of the situation helped boost his confidence. He could tell that this was a game of chess to Crowley, not a game of checkers, and he was intent on winning.

Chung proceeded to tell his side of the story, covering every detail of what he saw and observed. Crowley sat in silence and listened to every word as he laid it all out. Even when Chung's tone became overcome with fear as he talked about seeing the Hexies, the Malum, or over losing their friend, Crowley didn't waver and cut him off. He just let him speak and tell his side of the story.

Once Chung finished, Crowley said, "Jason, you can start telling your perspective of what happened, in detail, please. I need to hear your side even if some or most of the story is exactly the same. Do not worry about repeating the same things. I am more worried about hearing your personal observations than I am about being bored by repeated details. Leave nothing out."

Jason then proceeded in telling his perspective of what happened and everything he had seen. As he talked, JD took notice of the things Jason said, things that were slightly different than Chung's version of events, or things Chung had forgotten to mention. Things that could prove to be vitally important. He could tell, though, how shaken up they both were from what they'd seen.

Jason finished telling his side of the story just as they pulled into Castle Dale and into the café-motel they'd stayed at the night before. Crowley turned off the Chevelle's engine and paused for a moment, then said, "We leave at first light tomorrow. Chung and Jason, you will take position on top of the mesa and will observe everything in sight. If JD and I should die, I want you to make your way back to Harmonia's place and have her document everything you witnessed. I apologize, but you will have to walk the twenty-five miles back to Castle Dale on foot, as we will need the speed of the car when we attack. One more thing, come back to the trunk with me."

The three of them waited as Crowley opened the trunk, moved the spare tire, and they could now see there was a secret compartment underneath. As Crowley unlocked the secret compartment and lifted the door up, the boys were surprised to see multiple types of handguns, two rifles with scopes mounted on them, lots of ammo, and a few honest-to-God hand grenades.

"Jason and Chung, I want the two of you to each take one of these rifles with you when you go on top of the mesa. I understand you've probably never shot these types of rifles, or maybe any high-powered rifle for that matter, especially at these distances. I will give you both a crash course in how to use them tonight. Again, remember that a rifle or handgun will not kill a Hexies, but it will slow them down momentarily, which may be just the edge JD and I need to kill all of them before they kill us. All I ask is that you don't shoot JD or me."

Jason piped up and said, "Well, we have shot our .22 rifles a lot back home."

"Good, that will at least help with your breathing and trigger control. Let's go get something to eat and talk strategy," said Crowley.

They went inside and again sat at the booth that was the farthest away from anyone. After the same waitress as before came and took their order, Crowley laid down the entire plan in detail. After he was finished, the boys looked at each other and nodded their heads in agreement. They knew Crowley had really thought things through, and there might be a chance of success if they followed his instructions. They also knew there was no other choice. If not them, then whom? They each thought if they didn't try to stop the Hexies—which would hopefully result in killing the black pillar along with the Malum—then life was doomed as they knew it.

After dinner they went back to the Chevelle, grabbed the rifles, a few handguns, and some ammo. "It's now time for a crash course in modern-day weaponry, boys," said Crowley.

Once they were inside their motel room, Crowley handed Chung and Jason each a rifle, checking the action first and showing them that each rifle was empty. He then said, "This is a bolt-action Winchester .300 Magnum. It was first introduced by Winchester back in 1963. It's a flat shooter and packs a helluva punch. The scope mounted to each rifle is a Leupold 3X9X50. You'll be shooting 180-grain Winchester Powerpoint cartridges. Go ahead and pull out the ammo and feel its weight." He then grabbed one of the rifles from Jason and said, "I'm now going to show you boys how to load the rifle and cycle out the empty cartridges as you shoot. Keep in mind, I'm keeping the rifle on safety, as you can see here. An easy way to remember is red means danger, and black means safe. Probably similar to the .22s you boys used to shoot back home."

Jason and Chung nodded their heads that they understood.

Crowley then demonstrated how to load the rifle, fire it, then cycle through each round after they had fired. He also showed them how to adjust the magnification on the scope and explained why it would obviously be better to leave them both on nine power, since their shots would be from a long distance. He then handed the rifle back to Jason and told the boys to practice loading, aiming, and firing, but to make "damn sure" each rifle was on safety.

Crowley sat and watched them closely as they practiced cycling cartridges through the rifle, critiquing them along the way.

After spending the day prepping, and when he thought the boys had made some nice progress, Crowley said, "Boys, it's almost 11:00—let's get some shuteye. We'll be back at it by 6:00 again."

As always, Crowley grabbed his brown leather bag and began pouring out the black sand, making a circle around the beds. He then placed the black ram's skull painting in the middle of the circle, finishing with his chant. Once that was done, he flipped off the lights, and they were all out within seconds.

LXVI

JD was the first one of the boys to wake up. He looked over and noticed Crowley was cleaning up the black sand.

"Good to see you're waking up on your own now. It's almost 6:00, so wake up Jason and Chung," said Crowley.

"Hey, guys, it's almost 6:00—time to get up!" hollered JD, beginning to see why Crowley chose to wake them up that way every morning.

Jason and Chung both rolled over and immediately hopped out of bed. Adrenaline was already flowing through their veins at this point.

"Morning, boys! We leave after breakfast," said Crowley.

The boys got dressed and loaded the rifles and supplies into the Chevelle. By the time they went into the café for breakfast, they were starting to feel like they might be awake.

They all ordered the same breakfast, but this time there was an eerie silence as they ate. After they finished eating and paying the bill, Crowley took out his wallet, grabbed a hundred-dollar bill, and left it on the table as a tip. They then made their way to the Chevelle and piled in. Crowley fired up the engine and sped off down Main Street toward the mesa.

Everyone was still silent as they sped down the highway toward the mesa. As they got closer to where Crowley would park to let Jason and Chung out, he asked, "Are you boys ready for this?"

The two of them looked solemn but determined as they both answered, "Yes."

As Crowley pulled over and parked to let Jason and Chung out, he turned around to look at them. "We'll give you boys a good solid two hours to get into position before we make our way to the farm and execute our plan. Once we get within a certain distance of the farm, they will sense us coming, and that is when things will start to change. The jig will be up at that point, and there will be no turning back. Remember everything you've learned, and remember what to do if both of us should die. No matter what happens, though, I want you boys to know it was a pleasure getting to know each of you, and I thank you for doing this. I know this is the last place you want to be right now. If everything goes according to plan and we somehow survive, we will meet you both back here at the same spot. Good luck, fellas."

Crowley popped the trunk, and Jason and Chung each grabbed a rifle, the spotting scope, and other supplies, and started their journey toward the top of the mesa.

JD and Crowley sat quietly in the Chevelle for a while before speaking. "Are you ready for this? I understand you're probably scared as hell, and you wouldn't be human if you weren't, but use that fear to focus. Fear can do two things to you, it can either propel you into greatness and you can accomplish things you never knew you could, or it will paralyze you and you're dead. Focus on the plan, focus on killing them and nothing else. If you do that, fear will propel you to a level of greatness you would have never thought you were capable of," said Crowley.

"I'll be sure to do that. If we don't kill them, who else will?" replied JD.

"Yes, my boy! That's what I want to hear. I think you're ready to kick some ass and send some Hexies to hell, where they belong," responded Crowley.

"How much longer do we have?" asked JD.

Crowley looked at his watch. "One hour and twenty minutes until we fire up the Chevelle and execute our plan."

JD nodded his head and continued going over the plan and training in his mind again and again. He tried to keep his mind focused on what was most important right now, mapping out each detail that could mean the difference between success and . . . death.

Right then, Crowley opened up the car door, went to the trunk, and grabbed some food and drinks. When he came back and sat down, he threw JD a gas station sandwich and a can of Mountain Dew and said, "Eat and drink, boy. You'll need the energy."

"I have to say, Crowley, I sure as hell won't miss these goddamn gas station sandwiches."

Crowley let out a chuckle and said, "I hear ya there, boy. They do taste like something a rhino would shit out."

They both laughed and made small talk as they ate their sandwiches and drank their Mountain Dews. As JD watched his companion, he was somewhat surprised by how much he had grown to like Crowley, even though he'd only known him for such a short period of time. Maybe it was the thought of them facing death together, or the thought he might never see his own family again. That train of thought made him emotional and uneasy, and he tried to push it out of his mind and focus, like Crowley had told him to do. Once he refocused on the plan and the importance of killing Hexies, the thoughts of despair left his mind.

When the last hour went by and it was time to leave, Crowley looked at JD and said, "It's 10:45 a.m.—it is time, boy. Like I told Jason and Chung, it's been a pleasure getting to know you. I don't know what the future holds for us, but I hope it's something good. Remember, I got your back, and you got mine. We mustn't turn our backs on a Hexies for even a second."

Crowley then fired up the Chevelle, revved up the engine, put it into drive, and sped off, racing toward the Verwer farm. Neither one spoke as they got closer and closer to the farm. JD looked to the right as they passed the mesa that Jason and Chung were on top of. They then hit the dirt road that would lead them to the farm. In that moment, they both knew the Hexies would've sensed them, and there was no turning back.

LXVI

As the farm came into view just above the cornfield that was next to the dirt road, they could both see there was no one in sight. Crowley knew they were hiding, waiting for them—they were expecting this.

"We hit the barn first, just as planned. JD, light up the Molotov cocktail now, and get a grenade ready," said Crowley.

JD flicked the lighter on and lit the Molotov cocktail. He held it outside the window, ready to throw it on Crowley's cue. "Throw it now, boy!" yelled Crowley. JD threw it at the barn, breaking the bottle and sending flames up the side of it. Crowley turned the car hard left, making a half circle, and brought the Chevelle to a screeching halt within twenty feet of the barn, as gravel and dirt went flying into the air. JD immediately grabbed the grenade that was sitting between his legs, pulled the pin, hopped out of the car, and rolled the grenade in through a crack in the barn's front door.

BOOM! The grenade went off, sending parts of the wooden barn and straw flying all over the place.

Crowley came running around the back of the Chevelle to meet up with JD. Each of them immediately pulled out their H-blades, got into a fighting stance, and stood back-to-back with each other, ready to fight.

As they both stood there, waiting in suspense, they heard the loudest, most insane screeching JD could have possibly imagined. Both barn doors flew open with a crash, and out came three Hexies, running straight toward Crowley and JD. JD could see one of them was missing an arm, and another was missing half of its face, due to the shrapnel from the grenade.

"Get ready, boy! Here come three of them! Remember, focus on killing them and nothing else. They'll try surrounding us, and they'll come from all sides," yelled Crowley.

As the Hexies got closer and closer with each step, JD was running the plan of attack through his mind. When one of the Hexies got within a few feet of him, JD heard a loud *boom!* Then the Hexies in front of him screamed and flipped around like it'd just been hit by something. This was just the opportunity JD needed, and he lunged for the occipital artery with his H-blade, slicing it perfectly. The Hexies fell to the ground in a heap. JD then quickly backed up until he hit Crowley's back with his own. There was another loud *boom* and more screeching, and JD felt Crowley lunge forward, like he'd just done, then come right back into position. JD knew Crowley had just killed another one.

The third Hexies stopped dead in its tracks, threw out its arms so they could see its long claws as it screamed, and again, there was a loud *boom!* Only this time, this Hexies didn't waver but kept screaming, waiting to pounce. *Boom!* The next shot was a direct hit to the Hexies' head. JD watched as Crowley took advantage of the opportunity and, with fluid-like motion, moved to the back of the Hexies, plunging his H-blade into its artery. The Hexies immediately dropped to the ground.

Crowley quickly went back-to-back with JD again and said, "It's not over, boy, so don't let down your guard. There should be four more coming."

They stood waiting, in fighting stances, between the Chevelle and barn as it went up in a hellacious blaze. They knew the next wave of attacks would be coming soon.

It wasn't more than a few seconds later that JD could see the four other Hexies approaching from all different directions. Only this time, they weren't running. They seemed calm, walking smoothly and slowly. JD could see them baring their long claws as they approached.

"These ones are different, more dangerous. Be ready, boy!" said Crowley.

As the Hexies were approaching them from all sides, Crowley and JD heard two more loud *booms,* each one only a few seconds apart. They saw something hit the ground just behind one of the Hexies, sending dirt flying. Then, again, two more loud *booms*, just like before, only this time they found their mark, and they could see one of the Hexies stumble as it got hit. This didn't stop it, though—it kept approaching.

"Be ready. We're in for a good fight," said Crowley, his voice grim and determined.

The Hexies were now within ten yards of them, still slowly approaching. Crowley and JD readied and braced themselves.

Crowley turned his head slightly toward JD and said in a low voice, "Attack the ones that get hit by the rifles first, if you can. That will give you the split second you need to move behind them and slice the artery."

"Got it!" replied JD.

As the Hexies moved closer, they heard another *boom*, and the Hexies in front of Crowley stumbled. Crowley seized the opportunity to move behind the Hexies and kill it, but the other three Hexies thought just as quickly. Right as Crowley got done pulling his H-blade out of the Hexies neck, the other three pounced on JD. Crowley instantly sprang into action, running over and killing the Hexies closest to him. As he plunged his H-blade into the Hexies' artery, he could hear JD screaming for help.

The two other Hexies were on top of JD now, and he could feel their black nails digging into him, tearing at his flesh. He could feel the warmth of his blood as it escaped his body. He knew they were trying to reach his neck, but luckily, when they pounced, he had immediately curled into a fetal position, wrapping his arms over his head and squeezing tight. He was doing his best to protect his neck, having remembered what Crowley told him, that Hexies always go for the neck for a quick kill.

Crowley immediately went for the next one that was closest and dropped it in its tracks. As it fell, it landed on top of JD. The last Hexies saw this and immediately jumped back a few feet, into a fighting stance, its claws in the air, telling Crowley to stay back. Then, in the creepiest voice JD had ever heard, the Hexies said, "Hello, Crowley, we've been expecting you, you and your little friends on top of the mesa."

LXVI

Right then, they heard several shots being fired, one right after another—*boom, boom, boom, boom*! These shots sounded different than the ones before. They seemed to be going in a different direction, then, all of sudden, there was dead silence.

JD was still on the ground but didn't waste any time backing up toward Crowley as fast as he could move to get some distance between him and the Hexies. As he was backing up, he noticed the Hexies was smiling at Crowley, and before he could blink, Crowley was toe-to-toe with the Hexies. Each one struggled to kill the other. JD knew he had to do something, and he immediately began searching the ground for his H-blade.

After what seemed like minutes but was actually seconds, he found it, picked it up, and immediately lunged for the Hexies. He didn't have time to aim properly, and he hit the Hexies in the side of its body, just below the rib cage. The Hexies let out a blood-curdling scream, then backhanded JD across the face, sending him stumbling backward several feet. This would prove to be the last fatal mistake the Hexies would make because this distraction gave Crowley the split second he needed to get behind it and slice its artery. The Hexies dropped to the ground, and within seconds there was a large dark pool of blood forming in the dirt that started to surround its body.

JD looked over at Crowley and expected to see relief on his face, or maybe even a slight grin, because they'd just cheated death. What he saw instead was something he knew he would never forget. It was the look of pure dread and sadness.

"What, Crowley!" screamed JD.

Crowley just stood there, glaring down at the ground. It took him a minute to speak, and what he said next was the last thing JD was expecting, and definitely the last thing he would have wanted to hear. "Jason and Chung, those four shots fired on the mesa were not meant for the Hexies down here."

JD immediately knew what he meant and collapsed to the ground on his knees, overwhelmed by a feeling of utter emptiness. They'd missed a Hexies. It was on top of the mesa and had attacked Jason and Chung. Deep down, he knew that was true, but he didn't want to believe it. There was a slim chance they'd survived. At least, he would tell himself that.

Crowley walked over to the Chevelle and sat down on the ground, leaning against the passenger's side door, trying to catch his breath. JD was covered in Hexies blood and was also bleeding badly from the deep wounds the Hexies had inflicted on him. He didn't even notice because he was in a deep state of shock. The horrific thought of possibly losing his last two friends, his brothers, was beyond comprehension.

Crowley sat in silence against the Chevelle as the barn continued burning up in a towering blaze. He knew it was best to let JD gather himself. In their current state, there was nothing they could do for his friends, regardless if they were alive or dead. Crowley also knew the chances of them being alive were very small. He felt nothing but sadness for JD. He knew JD's life had been turned upside down since they'd met. Crowley had lived a good life, and he was always prepared to die at any moment. Seeing someone as young as JD go through this was not right. No kid, barely fifteen years old, should have to experience something so brutal, a loss so complete.

Several hours went by before JD spoke or even moved from the spot where he'd collapsed.

When he did finally speak, he asked, "Crowley, what more do we need to do here?"

"Nothing, other than get you bandaged up and get outta here before it gets dark. Otherwise, we'll have a helluva lot worse to deal with than the Hexies," replied Crowley.

Crowley finally stood up and went to the trunk of the Chevelle. He grabbed a first aid kit, brought it over to where JD was, and bandaged up his wounds. Most of the bleeding had stopped, but his wounds needed to be cleaned and sterilized.

"JD, I know this is going to be very difficult for you, but we need to drive over to where we were supposed to meet up with Jason and Chung, to see if they're there. If not, I need to hike to the top of the mesa to see exactly what happened," said Crowley.

JD said nothing. He just stood up, which in itself was difficult, having been in the same position for several hours. It didn't help that the deep gashes all over his body were making him stiff. He picked up his H-blade from the ground, where it had fallen several feet away, and moved over to the Chevelle. He climbed into the passenger seat and closed the door, staring straight ahead.

Crowley finished putting things away in the trunk then got behind the wheel. He turned the engine on without saying a word. There was nothing that he could say in this situation to help anything, so silence seemed the best choice.

As Crowley made a U-turn with the Chevelle to get onto the dirt road that would lead them back to the highway, JD noticed the black pillar sitting there and wondered if they had managed to kill it. All he could do was hope. There were still many unanswered questions going through his mind: *Was there another Hexies we missed? Are my friends dead? Will we be able to stop the Malum that has already entered our world?*

Once Crowley hit the asphalt highway going sixty miles per hour it jolted JD back to reality. All he could do was hope his friends were somehow still alive.

When the area came into view where they were supposed to meet Jason and Chung, they could see no one was there. JD's heart immediately sank, and he fought like hell to keep the tears from flowing. He didn't want Crowley seeing him cry like a baby, so he turned his head to look out the window. He happened to glance over at Crowley through the corner of his eye and saw what he thought was a single tear running down the man's cheek.

Crowley pulled the Chevelle over to the exact spot they'd previously parked and turned the car off.

"JD, this is not open for debate. You will wait here with the doors locked and a .45 revolver between your legs. I don't need to tell you what to do if someone shows up and tries to get into the car, do I? Also, make sure you keep your eye on the talisman. It'll tell you if someone's a Hexies or not," said Crowley.

Crowley paused for a moment, and JD could see he was struggling with his next sentence. "I know you're probably wondering why I didn't give the talisman to Jason and Chung? It only has a range of ten yards, so it wouldn't have mattered if they had it or not. If a Hexies was able to get within ten yards of them without being noticed, it might as well have been two inches," said Crowley.

"You don't need to explain yourself. I understand. I don't blame you for what happened. I'll wait here. I couldn't hike up the mesa even if I wanted to," replied JD.

"I'll leave the keys here with you as well, in case I never come back. If I'm not back by morning, you get the hell outta here and drive back to Harmonia's place. Is that understood?" said Crowley.

"Yes, understood," replied JD, his heart in his throat.

LXVI

Crowley got out of the car and went to the trunk. He reached down and grabbed a shiny silver Colt .45 revolver. He then came around to the passenger side, opened the door, and handed the revolver to JD along with the car keys.

"Lock the doors immediately," said Crowley. He then turned around and walked away, following the same path Jason and Chung had taken each time.

JD wasted no time locking the doors. He put the .45 between his legs with the barrel facing away from him.

There was a lot going through his mind as he watched Crowley walk away. It still seemed like he was living in a nightmare he couldn't wake up from. In that moment of despair, he decided he didn't want to be alive anymore. As tears streamed down his face, he looked down at the .45, his chest tight, and lifted it. He placed the barrel inside his mouth, cocked the hammer back, put his finger on the trigger, and told himself to squeeze it. But he couldn't do it. The only thing stopping him was the thought of his parents, that they might still be alive, and what it would do to them if they knew he had taken his own life. He wanted to hug the both of them one more time.

As JD was going through his own personal hell back in the car, Crowley was picking his way along the steep mountainside that led to the top of the mesa. He was being extremely careful not to get hurt, but at the same time, keeping his head on a swivel looking for the Hexies he knew had to still be in the area. The last thing he wanted was to get caught off guard.

Once he made it to the top, he knew he would be able to see for miles in every direction. He decided to take a few minutes and scan the surrounding area for the Hexies before proceeding to the area of the mesa where he assumed Chung and Jason would have been. After a few minutes of intently scanning the area and not seeing anything, he decided it was time to go find them. This was something he'd been dreading. Even though he'd seen a lot of horrific things in his lifetime, things that would make most people lose sleep for the rest of their lives, the one thing he never did get used to was seeing his friends die.

After a while of picking his way along the top of the mesa, he saw what looked like red. It was hard to tell what it was against the red sandstone rocks that made up most of the mesa. As he slowly and cautiously approached the red stains on the rocks, his heart sank. What he'd feared most had just come true. The mutilated bodies of Chung and Jason were sprawled out all over the red sandstone rocks. The rifles were a few feet from them, and there was spent brass all over the ground from the shots they'd fired. He quickly regained his composure and made a full circle, scanning the area, because he knew all too well this would be the best chance the Hexies had at catching him off guard. There were a lot of big boulders and small ravines on top of the mesa that the Hexies could hide in. He didn't want to get killed before he had a chance at killing this Hexies and avenging Jason and Chung.

Crowley walked over to the bodies, knelt down next to them, and put a hand on each of their foreheads. As tears rolled down his face, he whispered, "I'm very sorry this happened to you, my friends. I'll see you on the other side."

Crowley wished he could give them a proper burial, but he had no shovel and no time, as it was now getting late. It would also be dangerous for him to get distracted. After a few minutes of paying his respects, he picked up both rifles, the leftover ammo, and the spotting scope. With slow, methodical steps, he started to make his way back to the car.

The only thought going through his head now was how he was going to break the news to JD that his last two friends were now gone from this world. One other thought did go through his mind, though, and that was that it was going to be dark before he made it back to the Chevelle. This made Crowley nervous. There was still one other Hexies running around out here somewhere, and he was physically beat down from the fight earlier, on top of which he had hiked several miles up the mesa. He knew he had to heighten his senses as he hiked along, as this was his best and only defense in the dark.

As he hiked along in the dark, he carefully picked his way through the rocks and ravines that covered the desolate mesa. Adrenaline was flowing through his veins like a virgin on prom night. Having only a small handheld flashlight, which he didn't want to turn on for fear of alerting the Hexies to his location, he relied on the moon's light. He would pause at every sound, with his hand immediately going to his H-blade, and would listen intently. He was listening for the sounds only a human could make, but luckily, all he could hear so far were the sounds of coyotes barking in the distance and the occasional bird flying off when he got too close to it. Other than that, the silence was deafening.

After a while, Crowley finally made it to the edge of the mesa, to where he would descend through a narrow chute of cliffs, then on to flat ground. Not only was the descent steep and just keeping his balance would be challenging, but he knew this would be an opportune time for the Hexies to strike. Crowley knew he had to move extremely slowly as he made his descent, paying close attention as he took each step, then pausing to listen. It would take him a long time, but he knew he had no choice. He could not die, not yet.

He took a deep breath then took his first step.

While Crowley was weighing each move he made, JD was sitting in the car, passed out in a deep sleep from exhaustion. He was suddenly jolted awake by the loud sound of something scratching the side of the Chevelle. It sounded like someone was running a metal rake down the side of the car. JD quickly grabbed the .45 with his left hand and his H-blade with his right. As he did this, the scratching suddenly stopped. JD looked out the back window, then out the side windows to see what was making the noise, but it was pitch-black, and he could see nothing but darkness.

He sat there for several minutes, his heavy breathing the only sound, when, all of a sudden, the car started to violently shake, then something or someone grabbed the driver's side door handle, trying to get inside. As this was going on, the arrowhead talisman that was hanging from the rearview mirror lit up to a brilliant white color. JD knew then exactly what was trying to get inside the car. At this point, JD's instincts kicked in, and he readied himself for a fight. A furious rage started to surge through him as well. He knew this was the Hexies that had sneaked up on and likely killed his two best friends.

Without thinking, JD suddenly shouted at the Hexies with all he could muster, "Come on, you motherfucker! I'll fucking kill you! Open the door and see what happens, you son of a bitch!"

Immediately after JD finished shouting the last sentence, the shaking suddenly stopped. There was nothing but silence. It was so quiet, in fact, that JD could hear the loud beats of his heart as it hammered away in his chest.

LXVI

In the meantime, Crowley had safely made his way off the steep mesa and was now back on flat ground and within a quarter mile of the parked Chevelle. However, he was still slowly and carefully picking his way along as he walked, listening for any sound and stopping when he heard something.

As Crowley got closer to the Chevelle, the hairs on his arms stood straight up, and a chill went up his spine. He sensed something very evil was near, and he knew exactly what it was. He immediately dropped everything and reached for his H-blades.

He went into a fighting stance and yelled, "Show yourself, Hexies! I know you're out there!" Luckily, the moon was half full, shining enough light to see in the open area. He knew he still had to rely on his other senses in order to survive what was about to take place, but he was grateful for the illumination.

Right then Crowley heard the Hexies' creepy voice speak from somewhere in the darkness. "Hello, Crowley, son of Aleister. Did you find the present I left you on the mesa?" said the Hexies with a sinister laugh.

"Come at me, you evil bitch. I'll end your suffering right here, right now!" replied Crowley.

"You can't stop what's already begun, Crowley. You're too late. Embrace it," the Hexies said with a hiss from the darkness.

As they were going back and forth, Crowley was slowly spinning around, waiting for the quick attack he knew was coming. The Hexies would come at him strong and fast, and even a split second's delay could spell death for him.

Crowley now kept silent and focused his ears on any sound he could hear. By the sound of the Hexies' voice, he could tell it couldn't be more than fifteen to twenty yards away from him. This meant the Hexies could be on him in seconds.

Several long minutes of dead eerie silence went by, then Crowley heard the distinct sound of bare feet running up directly behind him.

Crowley instantly spun around and knew if this was like all the other Hexies, it would go for his neck. Crowley could hear the Hexies getting closer and closer, and he readied himself. When the Hexies got within a few yards of him, he could now see its shape under the light of the moon. Its arms were stretched out, its claws ready to tear at his flesh. Crowley held his position until the Hexies was less than a foot away, then he quickly sidestepped and countered with an elbow strike to the back of the head. This sent the Hexies stumbling forward in the air. Crowley quickly lifted his knee, placing it on the Hexies' back while it was in midair, then finished slamming the Hexies down to the ground as he thrust his H-blade into its occipital artery. "Time to go to hell, fucker!" he said. The Hexies let out the most hideous shriek then instantly went limp. Blood shot out of its artery, spraying Crowley in the face and covering most of his upper body in the Hexies' blood.

Crowley stood up, dripping in blood, H-blades still in both hands, trying to catch his breath. He'd just scorned death again. His thoughts then quickly went to JD, wondering if he was okay, hoping he was still alive. He was almost certain the Hexies had been to the Chevelle first.

Crowley put his H-blades back into their sheaths. He looked around for the flashlight that was still on the ground, picked it and the rifles and spotting scope up, and started to make his way onto the asphalt road and back toward the Chevelle.

The only thought that was going through Crowley's mind over and over as the Chevelle came into sight was, "Let the boy be alive, let the boy be alive." He walked straight to the passenger's side window, and he could see JD almost jump out of his seat as he got within a few feet of the window. This made Crowley burst out in laughter, not only from the huge sense of relief he felt knowing that JD was still alive, but he could imagine how he looked to JD, covered in the Hexies' blood.

JD rolled the window down and was half laughing when he said, "You son of a bitch, you scared the shit out of me. Why the hell are you covered in blood?"

"I had a close encounter with the last Hexies," replied Crowley.

"Doesn't surprise me. It paid me a visit not too long ago, but it couldn't get inside the car. I imagine it sensed you coming and went after you instead," said JD.

JD then asked Crowley the question he'd been dreading. "What about Chung and Jason? Are they . . . ?"

Crowley took a deep breath, and as gently as he could say it, he replied, "I'm sorry, boy, but they're both gone."

JD turned back in his seat to face forward. He said nothing as tears rolled down his face. Crowley knew it was better to say nothing than trying to find words of comfort, because there were no words that would help.

Crowley went to the back of the Chevelle, popped the trunk, and put away the rifles and spotting scope. He paused for a minute, deep in thought, feeling sorry for JD. A few minutes went by before he hopped behind the wheel and re-situated the car, heading south down the desert highway toward Harmonia's place in the Sonoran Desert.

LXVI

It was several hours before either of them spoke, and then it was only when they stopped at a gas station to fill up and get something quick to eat. "I'll grab you something to eat, boy. You can stay in the car," said Crowley as he hopped out.

Time was of the essence. Even though the Verwer Hexies were all dead, they still had the Malum to contend with.

When Crowley got out, he started filling up the car with gas then went inside to pay and grab some sandwiches and drinks. When he came back, he handed JD a sandwich and drink and said, "Go ahead and eat and drink whenever you feel up to it. This is the last stop we'll make before we make it back to Harmonia's place. We should be there in about five hours."

JD said nothing as he took the food. He was still in shock and still mourning over the death of his friends. He just wanted to be left alone, and Crowley, of course, knew the feeling all too well.

The sun was just starting to peek over the horizon as they made it to the old dirt road in the desert that would take them straight to Harmonia's shack. JD again noticed the sign with the black circle and ram's skull as Crowley made a hard right, leaving the asphalt for dirt.

JD's stomach started growling, startling him. He decided to open the sandwich and soda Crowley had bought for him, realizing how long it had been since he had anything to eat. Having food hit his stomach made him feel a little bit better, and he let out a sigh of relief. JD didn't notice, but Crowley also let out a sigh of relief. This wasn't Crowley's first rodeo, and he knew all too well that some people don't mentally come back from what JD had experienced. If JD happened to be one of those people, they would have a real issue. Not only did he like the boy and hope good things for his future, but he was also still going to need JD's help for what was to come in the present.

The Hexies were easy compared to the Malum. At least Hexies were flesh and blood and could be killed. Crowley had no idea how to deal with the Malum, or even what it was exactly. He only knew they were dark evil and came from another realm.

The sun was hitting the desert floor as they pulled up to Harmonia's shack. As Crowley stopped the engine, they looked over at Harmonia, who was coming outside. JD noticed she was looking at the backseat, then she slowly closed her eyes and dropped her head. She knew exactly what had happened to Jason and Chung.

As they got out of the car and approached Harmonia, she grabbed JD by the shoulders, looked him straight in the eyes, and said, "I'm very sorry, JD. There's nothing more that needs to be said."

JD just nodded his head. Nothing anyone could say could ease the pain he was feeling or bring his friends back from the dead, but he did appreciate her kindness.

Harmonia then looked at Crowley and said, "Let's go inside, men. I've been intently reading through your mother's journal's, Aleister, and I hope I've found the answer that will kill the Malum. However, I do hope to hell in a handbasket that killing those godforsaken Hexies killed the black pillars as well, or we may all be screwed."

As they walked inside, they saw there were journals spread out all over the place. "Have a seat, and I'll grab the journal that might hold the answer we're looking for," said Harmonia.

JD and Crowley sat down at the table across from each other as Harmonia walked into another room to grab the journal. When she came back, she sat down next to Crowley and laid the journal on the table. She opened it up to a specific page that had a drawing of a Malum and a page of text below it. Harmonia looked at them both and said, "I'll read aloud what it says, so don't interrupt me. It's important you listen closely and form your own opinion, then we'll discuss it later.

"It reads as follows: I've been studying the Malum for as long as I can remember. I've tried to learn how it came to be, how it enters our world, and how to destroy it, if it does in fact ever enter our realm. The most insightful information we've ever received regarding the Malum was from two different Hexies we captured, tortured, and extracted some information from. Of all the hundreds of years good witches and gifted ones have been killing Hexies, we've only been able to capture and keep two alive.

"The first capture was in the year 1704 in Transylvania, Romania, and the second capture was in 1836 in Klagenfurt, Austria. Even with the information we extracted from them, how do we trust it wholeheartedly? Unfortunately, it's the only information we have to go on. We did learn that when a Hexies creates a black pillar, their energy and life source are tied to it, thus killing the Hexies that created it may make it possible to kill the black pillar itself, thereby not allowing a gateway for the Malum to enter our realm. The Hexies would not outright divulge whether or not that was the case, but by their unwavering silence when asked that question, even after being tortured for days on end, we all agreed we could safely assume a black pillar that is created by a Hexies would die *enough* when they died. We did learn that one black pillar can only release one Malum.

"Both Hexies were asked how to stop a Malum once its entered our realm of existence. When asked, both Hexies slightly grinned then laughed and said almost exactly the same thing: 'You simple fools can never stop a Malum once it's entered this realm.' However, not believing them, we pushed and pushed for an answer, and only one Hexies muttered one word before dying from the torture. The other one simply died. The word the Hexies muttered was, *pillar*. Having heard that, we assumed the black pillar was the key to killing a Malum once it has entered our realm.

"I spent a good portion of my early life in Hammerfest, Norway, living deep in the forest next to and guarding a black pillar. I spent most of my days studying it, trying to figure out ways we could destroy it should the day come a Malum managed to get released into this world. Several things I noticed, even with the Hexies that created it being dead, at night, the black pillar would still give off an ever so slight amount of energy that I could feel, and it had almost a strange dark glow about it. The texture also became somewhat softer at night than in the day. In the daytime the pillars are rock-hard, as I and many others have tried smashing them and breaking them during the daylight hours and could not put so much as a scratch on them. I came to the conclusion it might be most vulnerable during the nighttime, when the pillar is softer, if it does in fact even have any vulnerabilities at all. If you're reading this, then you may wonder why I never tried destroying it at night? Again, I had no idea what would've happened if I'd tried. For example, would a Malum be released into our realm if the pillar were to be broken? Or would the pillar destroy me? We had no idea what to expect, so to not act seemed prudent. That, and there was no urgency back then. As I finish the writings on this subject years later, I wish I'd tried for the sake of knowing. Everything I write is, of course, theory, based on what little knowledge we do have.

"One last interesting fact we learned from those two Hexies, something we've been questioning and wondering about for some time, is they're forbidden to kill using other than their own hands—no knives, guns, or weapons of any kind. We don't know why, but that's what they told us.

"The notes from your mother on this subject stop there," said Harmonia.

"So there might be a chance at stopping the Malum or Malums that have already entered our world? Now we just need to figure out how and when to destroy the both of them," said Crowley.

"Well, the sooner the better, before it consumes every living thing on this continent. I've been thinking about this since I read your mother's journal entry, and I would suggest, based off of your mother's notes, that you should strike the pillar the very second the sun goes down. Once it gets too dark, you're obviously dead if there's a Malum in the area, which you can bet your tall, skinny ass there will be. Doing it in that split second the sun goes down may give you the time you need to destroy it, even if it is a second or two. We can only hope that when the sun goes down, the pillar might become vulnerable. As far as how to destroy the cursed thing, I would recommend dousing it in gasoline, lighting it on fire for thirty seconds before the sun goes down, then smashing it back to hell with a sledgehammer," said Harmonia.

Crowley nodded his head and said, "Yes, we hope anyways, right?"

"Yes, of course, my dear boy. It's the only thing we have to go on, and our only chance of killing the goddamned thing before it kills us and everything," replied Harmonia.

JD sat silently as they talked, only intently listening. He knew he was too much of a novice to have an opinion on the subject.

"Looks like we're headed back to Maine to destroy the first black pillar," said Crowley as he looked at JD.

"Yeah, I figured as much. I was thinking the same thing as you guys were talking," replied JD.

LXVI

JD was torn about heading back home, though. He did want to see if his parents were alive or if they'd safely made it out of Maine. He figured they would've absolutely left a note for him, but he wasn't sure he wanted to know the answer because it might not be what he was hoping for.

"We'll go back to Utah to the Verwer farm first and destroy that one, since it's closer, then we'll make the long journey back to Maine. We'll rest here for a few days, though, to let your wounds heal. I'll need your help, and going back freshly wounded would only undermine things," said Crowley.

JD nodded his head in agreement, then went back to his thoughts as Harmonia and Crowley continued talking.

JD spent the next few days resting, eating, and keeping mostly to himself. Crowley and Harmonia left him alone as well because they knew he needed space.

The night before they were going to leave, Crowley came into the room where JD was lying down on a cot and said, "Boy, we leave for Utah tomorrow at 5:00 a.m. We'll strike the black pillar at dusk, precisely as the sun sets. Come now and get some dinner. Harmonia made something special for our last night here."

JD got up, and they both walked into the kitchen to see Harmonia putting the final touches on dinner. "This here, men, is a special marinated coues deer steak. I killed, gutted, and skinned the little sucker myself. These tenderloin steaks have been marinating for the last twenty-four hrs in an old Greek sauce. The recipe has been handed down through my family for generations," said Harmonia.

As they ate dinner, the mood was light. They talked and joked as Harmonia told them stories of when she was a young tracker in Europe and all the crazy things she'd seen and experienced over a lifetime.

JD smiled as he listened to her stories and thought, *Not long ago, no one would've believed Harmonia if she'd told them these stories. They would've dismissed her as being an old, batshit crazy lady who is off her rocker, one who needs to be committed to a mental asylum. Now, however, it would be a different story because of what has been happening out East.*

When they finished eating dinner, Harmonia said, "Go to bed, boys, and I'll clean up. You'll need your rest for what lies ahead."

They didn't need to be told twice. Crowley and JD both stood up without saying a word and retired to their beds, quickly falling asleep.

JD woke up before Crowley could wake him. His mind was spinning, even at 4:30 in the morning. There was a lot going through his head, and he was still in disbelief over everything that had happened since it all started. It was like screaming to yourself to wake up from a nightmare, but no matter what you do, you can't wake up. He laid there in bed until he could hear Crowley moving around, then he got up and got dressed before Crowley could come into his room.

When Crowley came to get him, JD was sitting on the cot. Crowley flipped the light on and said, "You ready, boy?"

"As ready as I'll ever be," replied JD.

Crowley turned and headed straight for the front door, making his way outside to his trusty black Chevelle with JD in tow. JD noticed Harmonia wasn't present as they left, and he didn't feel like asking Crowley where she was. It didn't matter at this point.

They both climbed in, fired up the car's engine, and took off for Utah once again. As they left, both of them were wondering if they'd ever be able to come back to Harmonia's place and see her again.

As they started speeding along that empty desert road, Crowley said, "As you well know by now, we have a long drive to Utah before the sun sets. I'll be driving quite fast the entire time, stopping only for gas and food. Please keep your eyes open for the police, as getting pulled over will only slow us down. That, and I don't want to get questioned why we're carrying so many weapons, some of which are illegal for civilians to have."

"Of course, I'll be on the lookout," replied JD.

It was a clear, sunny day as they raced along the highway toward Utah. The roads were empty as they sped along, and it seemed as if they were the last two people on the planet.

The closer they got to Utah the more uneasy JD started to feel. At least Hexies were real human beings, something he could reach out and touch, but a Malum was something entirely different. To him they were something that was not real, and he wouldn't have even believed they existed if he hadn't seen one kill his friend with his own eyes.

As they passed the sign that said they were now entering Utah, JD felt a wave of darkness come over him. In that moment, Crowley looked over at him, and JD knew he'd felt it as well. After several more hours of driving, the mesa his friends had died on came into sight. The same dark, sickening feeling JD had felt when his friends died that night came rushing back, hitting him like a fist to the face.

Crowley looked over at him and said, "Be strong, boy. I know it's hard, but your mind must be focused right now."

As Crowley said that, JD was fighting back the tears and trying to keep his head up. JD knew Crowley was right. It would accomplish nothing if he got them both killed. After seeing what the Malum did to his friend Matt, and hearing his blood-curdling screams, he knew for certain he did not want to suffer the same excruciating death.

As the Chevelle sped closer and closer to the farm, the dark, evil feeling seemed to get stronger and stronger. The sun was only going to be in the sky for a little while longer, so it was do or die at this point. They then hit the dirt road that led to the farm, and it was only a matter of a few minutes now until the farm and black pillar would come into sight.

Crowley smashed the accelerator harder with his foot as they got closer. The farm then came into view, along with the black pillar, and the dead bodies of the slain Hexies. The Chevelle came screaming into the open area of the farm as Crowley did a full circle around the black pillar, sending dirt and rocks flying everywhere. He then hit the brakes, coming to a screeching halt.

"Let's move, boy! We only have a few minutes until the sun sets behind the cliffs," said Crowley as he jumped out of the car and made a beeline for the Chevelle's trunk.

JD, on the other hand, carefully got out of the car, slowly shut the car door, and just stood there about ten feet away from the black pillar, waiting. Crowley grabbed a red gas can from the trunk, walked over to the black pillar, and doused it, using every drop of gasoline from the can. He then tossed the gas can as far away from them as he could, reached into his pocket for a book of matches, lit one up, then lit up the rest of them. He paused for a few seconds before he threw the lit book of matches at the black pillar, sending flames spiraling ten feet up in the air.

LXVI

As JD stood there watching the flames climb higher and higher, Crowley had gone back to the trunk to grab something. When he came back, he was standing right next to JD. JD turned to look at Crowley, who was standing there holding a six-foot-long chainsaw with both hands.

Crowley looked at JD with a slight grin and said, "I want some distance between me and that mother." He then fired up the chainsaw, gunned it, and said, "Let's hope to hell this works or we're dead, my boy."

JD stood there with a bewildered look on his face, a bit surprised. He hadn't expected Crowley to bring out a six-foot chainsaw from the trunk, let alone bring it along without JD noticing. Crowley saw the look on his face and said, "My mother's journal said the pillar gets slightly softer at night, so it wouldn't make sense to use a sledgehammer. I'm going to cut the son of a bitch down!"

Crowley turned his head back to look at the position of the sun in the sky. He then yelled at JD over the roar of the chainsaw, "Only a minute or two now, boy. You need to let me know the second the sun is out of sight. If we don't time this just right, we're dead."

JD didn't have to be told twice. He quickly turned around to where he was facing the sun and his back was to the black pillar. He did this for two reasons: one, he wanted to see the very second the sun left the sky, and two, if it didn't work and they were going to be torn apart and consumed by the Malum, he didn't want to witness it head-on. He was going to close his eyes, let it happen, and fade to black. He was tired, tired from traveling, tired of losing his friends, and tired from the emotional roller-coaster he'd been on since all this shit started.

Crowley could see the look on JD's face and knew exactly what the young boy was thinking and feeling. He rested his hand on JD's shoulder for a brief second, letting him know he understood, and he felt the same way. He then put his hand back on the chainsaw and gunned it again, making sure it wouldn't shut off unexpectedly, something chainsaws are notorious for doing from time to time.

JD stood there watching the sun, waiting for it to disappear behind the red desert cliffs. It seemed like an eternity that he stood there, waiting.

As the last bit of sun crept behind the cliffs, JD shouted out, "Now, Crowley!"

Crowley gunned the chainsaw full throttle as he started cutting the black pillar at the very bottom. As he started cutting it and broke through, a thick, black liquid substance came squirting out, showering the both of them. Crowley maintained his focus despite the mess, holding on to the chainsaw with all his might as it growled through the black pillar. Crowley could see it was actually working and was cutting through. As he was halfway through the pillar, both JD and Crowley heard the loudest, most horrific scream, worse than any of the Hexies' screams. It was as if something or someone was getting cut in half along with the black pillar. It was the most god-awful scream they'd ever heard, and they could tell it was getting closer and closer to them.

"Crowley! Crowley! Hurry! Hurry!" screamed JD. Crowley said nothing. He knew exactly what he was hearing—he simply maintained his focus, letting the chainsaw do its job.

They could tell whatever was screaming was within yards of them now, drawing closer and coming fast. Crowley could see he only had a few centimeters left and pushed the chainsaw as hard as he could, finally cutting through the last of it. As the saw tore through the last bit of the pillar, the tool went flying out of his hands, hitting the dirt a few yards away. He'd been pushing so hard, he hit the dirt as well with a thud. As the chainsaw was flying through the air, the screaming instantly stopped as well. Crowley quickly stood up and did a 360, expecting to see death approaching, but there was nothing, nothing but dead silence and darkness.

Crowley stood there sucking air, trying to catch his breath. He was also trying to comprehend what had just happened. He was fully prepared for death and the fact that it might not work. Being alive was actually a surprise to him. He'd always lived by the mantra of hope for the best, plan for the worst.

After a few minutes went by, Crowley said, "Boy, let's go clean this shit off of us. Lord knows what it is."

JD was in shock that they were both alive as well. He looked at Crowley and just nodded his head.

"Come on, let's go inside the house and see if they have some rags we can use," said Crowley.

They started walking toward the house. It was getting somewhat dark, and there was a strange eeriness in the air as they walked closer to the house. As they got within a few yards, JD, who was behind Crowley, saw him reach behind his back and grab both of his H-blades. JD didn't hesitate and grabbed his as well.

The side door to the house was wide open. Crowley stopped before going inside, turning back to JD to say, "Boy, we're going to take it nice and slow. I need you to keep an eye on what's behind us."

"Got it," replied JD.

As they slowly entered the house through the side door, Crowley found the first light switch on the wall just to the left and flicked it on. Crowley started scanning the room for anything that might pose a threat. Then he slowly proceeded forward, toward the kitchen, with JD following. At this point JD was walking backwards, to make sure nothing came up behind them.

Once they made it to the kitchen, Crowley looked for the light switch and flicked it on. What they saw left them both in a state of horror. There were human body parts and blood everywhere.

When Crowley did finally speak, he said, "There's no question as to what happened in here, boy. Don't look away or ever forget this. This is the evil and reality we're dealing with."

"Crowley, you can bet your ass I won't ever forget. I'll never forget anything I have seen since this all started."

"Come on, let's check the other rooms for some rags or something to wipe us down with," said Crowley.

They continued moving slowly through the rest of the house, checking each room until they found one that had some old rags lying on the floor. They wiped off the thick black liquid from their faces, necks, and arms, making sure to get it all.

The house had the thick, pungent smell of death that made it difficult to breathe. There were also all kinds of strange writings, symbols, and scribblings on the walls.

"A lot of these writings are in Latin, and what they translate to are insane. You probably wouldn't believe me if I told you. I wish we had time to write it all down in a journal, but time is of the essence. If we actually survive this ordeal, we'll come back here and take scrupulous notes. Now, however, we must go. We have a long drive back to Maine," said Crowley.

With that being said, they both calmly walked back to the Chevelle, not caring at all about leaving the lights on in the house as they left. Crowley went over, picked up the chainsaw and gas can, and loaded them in the trunk. They each took a deep breath and one last look at the burnt-down barn, the multiple dead bodies, and the sawed-off black pillar. What had just happened all seemed so surreal to the both of them. The fact they were both still alive was a blessing, and an unexpected one. They climbed into the Chevelle. Crowley fired up the engines and sped off down the now-familiar dirt road that would lead them to the highway.

LXVI

As they were speeding along in the dark, Crowley said, "We're going to have to fly like a bat of hell as we make our way back to Maine. We have a long journey and, of course, no time."

"I understand. If you need me to drive at any point, let me know. I don't have a driver's license, but I've actually 'borrowed' my parents' car a few times," replied JD.

Crowley didn't say anything; he just smiled. He'd been young once, and JD saying that brought back good memories of his youth.

When they hit asphalt Crowley turned the Chevelle right this time, heading north instead of south. This highway would connect them to the freeway that would then take them east. They were essentially going back the same way they'd initially come.

JD started thinking about his parents. He was both excited and scared at the same time, not knowing what to expect when they made it back to his hometown. He kept hoping they were somehow still alive. He was also wondering how in the hell he was going to break the news to Jason's and Chung's parents that their children were dead.

His mind was racing as quickly as the Chevelle as they sped along that dark highway.

It didn't take long for JD to pass out. He was awoken to the sun hitting his face, and he jolted himself awake and blurted out without thinking, "Where the hell are we?"

"We're a few miles from the Kansas border, boy. You've been out for quite some time. I stopped and got some gas, food, and drinks while you were sleeping. They're in the backseat if you're hungry or thirsty. There's a rest stop coming up soon, and I'm going to stop to take a quick piss. If you need to as well, you'd better go while we're there."

"Hell yes. I need to piss like a racehorse," replied JD.

Crowley smirked, exiting the freeway and pulling into the rest stop.

They could see they were the only ones there, and they both quickly got out and made a beeline toward the restroom. Once they relieved themselves, they walked straight back to the car without uttering a word.

They were both exhausted, and each wanted to be left alone to their own thoughts.

Crowley fired up the Chevelle again and took off racing down the freeway, heading due east. The sun was now fairly high in the sky, and JD realized he was starving and thirsty. He reached in the backseat and grabbed the sandwich and Gatorade Crowley had bought for him.

After he finished eating and drinking, he felt a lot better, and his mind started racing again. JD soon realized that worrying and thinking about everything, again, wasn't going to help the situation. So he started looking out the window at his surroundings and just tried to live in the moment versus agonizing over what might be in store for them or what may have happened to his parents. This was country he'd never seen before and might never again, and he knew it. He may as well take in the scenery.

They drove all day until it was dark. When they were halfway through Kentucky, Crowley said, "Let's stop and get some dinner, boy."

JD nodded his head in acknowledgment. He needed to use the restroom again anyway.

They pulled into a Circle K gas station that was just off the freeway. Anytime they stopped for food Crowley would fill up the Chevelle at the same time, so it meant less stops along the way. They were making good time, but they had to keep pushing. As JD walked into the gas station and headed toward the restroom, he could see the news on the TV. Of course, the news was reporting about whole towns and cities of people who were disappearing at night without a trace. Seeing this now didn't faze JD at all, since he knew exactly what it was and how to stop it. His only concern was his parents and hoping they were still alive.

JD finished up as Crowley walked into the restroom to relieve himself also.

"Get us some food and drinks, and I'll meet you back at the car. Grab me a Snickers bar too, boy! I got a hankering to satisfy my sweet tooth," said Crowley.

"You got it," replied JD.

JD left the restroom and grabbed some food, drinks, and two Snickers bars, figuring he would get one for himself as well—he always had liked Snickers bars. As he was walking toward the counter to pay, he mumbled under his breath how much he wouldn't miss gas station food and was frankly fed up with eating this "shit."

He could see Crowley was already sitting in the driver's seat with the engine humming when he left the store. The second JD got in, Crowley put the car into drive and laid a patch of rubber out of the parking lot as they sped back to the freeway entrance.

"Here's your food, drink, and Snickers bar, as requested," said JD as he handed them to Crowley.

"Thanks, boy. I don't normally eat sweets, but I figured what the hell, right? And Snickers bars are my favorite."

Crowley opened the Snickers bar first and devoured it rather quickly. JD, on the other hand, wanted his ham-and-egg sandwich first and was saving the Snickers bar for later.

They continued driving for what seemed like days before they finally saw a sign saying they were now entering Vermont. The city of Burlington, to be exact.

"We're only about six hours from Bangor, Maine, now, boy. We'll drive to the city of Waterbury, which is about another thirty minutes, and spend the night there. We'll then wake up early and time it just right so we enter the infected area at light. It hasn't spread to Waterbury yet, but it is getting close. Of course, we don't want to drive through the infected area during dark. If I've timed it correctly, that should give us plenty of time to drive to Bangor and hike to the Smith Cemetery. We'll be in position well before the sun sets behind the mountains," said Crowley.

"Got it, but can we please eat at a real restaurant tonight? I can't stomach another gas station sandwich, and this may be our last hot meal."

"Of course, boy."

When they pulled into the city of Waterbury, Crowley asked, "Where would you like to eat?"

"I want a big, juicy steak with a baked potato with everything on it," replied JD.

"Sounds good to me. Let's find us a steakhouse," said Crowley.

They drove down Main Street until they saw a neon sign that said: *Joe Bob Birgg's Steak and Lobster House.*

As they pulled into the parking lot, they could see it was open, but there wasn't anyone else there, though this didn't surprise them much. Most people were probably getting the hell outta town at this point, fleeing for the West to escape the darkness that was spreading.

When they opened the doors and went inside, they were greeted warmly by a young, beautiful blonde waitress who was most likely in her early twenties.

She smiled and said, "Hi there! Welcome to Joe Bob Birgg's Steak and Lobster House. Would you guys like a booth? We got plenty of open ones."

"Yes, ma'am," replied Crowley.

She led them to a booth by the big window in front and handed them menus as they sat down.

"We have tons of food we need to get rid of, so you'll get double of whatever you order for the price of one meal," said the waitress.

"Sure, that sounds great! We haven't had a good, hot-cooked meal for a few days," replied JD.

She smiled and said, "Great, guys, just holler at me when you're ready to order. My name is Diana."

"Thank you, Diana, we will. I see on your nametag that it says Diana P. What does the P stand for, if you don't mind me asking?" asked Crowley.

"It stands for Poulsen—my last name is Poulsen," replied Diana with a smile. She then turned around and walked back toward the kitchen and disappeared into the back somewhere.

"Well, it won't take me long to decide. I'll have the house steak special with the baked potato," said JD.

"Me too, boy, but I'm going to toss in a big mug of the local beer to wash it down with," said Crowley.

He then turned to look behind him and shouted, "Diana, we're ready to order."

"Sounds good, hon, I'll be right there," she shouted back.

She came back carrying her pen and pad and said, "What can I get you guys?"

"We'll both take the house steak special with the baked potato, and I'll get a mug of the local beer," said Crowley.

"Sure thing, guys, and I'll get that beer right out to you. The local beer is great, by the way. You'll love it."

"Good to hear. I look forward to trying it." Crowley flashed a slight grin.

Diana walked back to the kitchen and came back a few minutes later with Crowley's mug of beer.

"Just holler at me if you guys need anything, but your meals should be out before too long," she said.

This time JD spoke and said, "Thank you, Diana, we'll let you know."

JD waited until Diana was out of sight before he spoke again. "I sure hope this isn't the last steak we ever get to eat."

"You and me both, boy. Things don't always go according to plan, but we have no other choice. I've been sensing since we've been getting closer to Maine that something is off, something different than the Verwer farm. Part of our gift is sensing evil, so I know to take it seriously. There's definitely something different. I believe something beyond what we expect is waiting for us," said Crowley.

Hearing that didn't make JD feel any more comfortable. He knew what Crowley meant because he'd been sensing it too as they got closer. He was trying to dismiss it as nothing, but now Crowley just confirmed it.

LXVI

A few minutes went by, and it wasn't long before Diana came back carrying their plates of food. "Here you go. I know it's a lot of food, guys, so don't worry if you can't finish it all."

"This steak sure does look good enough to eat. Thank you, Diana. My compliments to the chef," said Crowley.

"Well, you're very welcome, hon. I'll let the chef know. He likes hearing things like that," replied Diana before she went back to the kitchen.

"Damn, you're right, this does look good. Can't wait to sink my teeth into it," said JD.

They both started to devour their dinner like it was going to be their last meal, which might not be too far from the truth. They savored each delicious bite as much as possible.

When they finished eating everything on their plates, Crowley reached for his wallet, opened it up, and pulled out two crisp hundred-dollar bills. Setting them down on the table, he said, "Let's go, boy. We need some shuteye before tomorrow's reckoning."

They got up and walked out of the restaurant and toward the car without ever seeing Diana again. They were both secretly hoping to get one more glimpse of the blonde beauty, and they couldn't help feeling a bit disappointed that she stayed out of sight.

They drove through the main stretch of town, which at this point looked more like a ghost town than a thriving city. After a few minutes, they spotted a local motel. Crowley pulled the Chevelle into the parking lot and parked in front of the office. They could see someone standing behind the counter, and there were no other cars parked at the motel.

JD and Crowley got out and walked into the front office. The person behind the counter was a man probably in his thirties, and they both noticed he had a somewhat surprised look on his face when he saw them.

"Wow, I never expected anyone to check-in tonight. As a matter of fact, I'm pulling up anchor and getting the hell outta here tomorrow morning," said the man.

"We hear that. We're only staying tonight, then we're leaving the city tomorrow as well," replied Crowley.

JD didn't say anything, he just kept his mouth shut. He knew saying less was better. They couldn't tell anyone what they were actually doing. Who would believe them?

Crowley reached for his wallet and took out another hundred-dollar bill and handed it to the man. "Here you go. You can keep whatever is left over for yourself."

"Why, thank you, mister, that's mighty nice of you. Here's your key. You'll be in room number seven. It's within walking distance just over to the right," said the man as he pointed to their room.

"You're welcome, and again, thank you. We'll just leave the key in the room when we check out tomorrow," said Crowley.

"Sounds good. You both have a good night, and good luck to you," said the man.

When they walked outside toward the car, JD asked, "He didn't seem too panicked, did he? Why is that?"

"Over the years of my life, I've noticed there are two types of people when faced with death, the unknown, or high-stress situations. They either handle it very well or push it out of their minds, but either way, they're calm and cool and will actually perform amazing feats. The other type either panics and dies, or they lose their minds. It seemed to me that both Diana and that man fall into the category of being calm and cool. The other thought that came to my mind was that they're somehow in on it, as unlikely as that sounds. Of course, they're not Hexies themselves, but they may be helping the Hexies. We'll be setting up the BWC—Black Witches Circle—tonight, but we need to take turns keeping watch. If they are helping the Hexies, then we won't be able to sense them coming, which gives them the element of surprise. That makes them dangerous if we're both asleep."

"Got it," replied JD.

After grabbing their stuff from the Chevelle, they walked over to their room. After they were inside, they locked and bolted the door, shut the blinds, then pushed the single beds together so they could set up the BWC. After they finished setting up the BWC, they talked briefly about the plan for the following day. They planned on waking up at 7:00 a.m., when it would be light enough outside. Then, they would drive like a bat out of hell toward Bangor. They weren't sure exactly how far the darkness had spread, and they didn't want to run into an affected area by mistake while it was still dark. Crowley decided to take first watch. JD laid down on the bed. Once his head hit the pillow, he was out in a matter of seconds.

About four hours later, JD was awakened to Crowley grabbing him by the shoulder and saying, "It's time, boy. Make sure to wake me up in four hours. Keep this .357 pistol in your hands or lap at all times. If you hear something or start to sense that something is off, no matter how small of a feeling it is, you must wake me up immediately. I brewed you some fresh coffee; it's over there, on the table."

JD, who was still in somewhat of a daze, stood up, got off the bed, and nodded his head to Crowley. He stumbled over to the table to grab the much-needed cup of coffee. He turned around and picked up the .357 pistol from the chair then sat down and began sipping his coffee. After a few minutes, the fuzziness in his mind started to clear with the help of coffee. As he was sipping, he looked over at Crowley, who was dead asleep by now and was starting to snore. JD started thinking how fond he'd grown of Crowley since their first meeting. At this point, he thought of him not only as a good friend but as family.

This made him start thinking about his parents. He wasn't sure what he might or might not find when he got back home. Not knowing the answer to that question had actually been helping his mindset, but he was going to find out tomorrow, whether he wanted to or not.

LXVI

After he finished his first cup of coffee, he went over and poured himself another cup. He knew how important it was for him to stay awake, and it would only take a few seconds to fall fast asleep. He knew he'd have to continue drinking coffee until morning, needing the jolts from the caffeine in order to keep watch. Right as he was pouring his second cup of coffee, he heard the whisper of that creepy voice he'd heard when this all started, and again, it used his first name and not his nickname. "James . . . James . . . join me or die," it hissed.

JD immediately flipped around, dropping his cup of coffee in the process. As his cup hit the floor, he was jolted awake and jumped out of the chair with the .357 hitting the floor. As he stood there, shaking, breaking out in a sweat, his gaze went to the .357 that was now on the floor. He realized that he had fallen asleep and had been having the nightmare again. He turned to look at Crowley, who, amazingly, was still fast asleep, even with the loud thud of the pistol hitting the floor.

JD made the decision it was best to stay standing up until morning, and he decided he would also drink as much coffee as his stomach and bladder could stand. He spent the rest of the night pacing the room, watching the clock and consuming endless cups of coffee.

When the clock hit 7:00 a.m. on the dot, JD went over to Crowley, grabbed his shoulder, and said, "Crowley, it's seven—time to go. I have some coffee and food prepared for you."

"Thanks, boy. Looks like those two weren't in on it after all, which is good. They seemed like genuinely good people, and I didn't want to have to kill them," said Crowley.

While Crowley was talking, JD went and grabbed Crowley's cup of coffee and came back and handed it to him. Crowley took the cup and nodded to JD as he took a sip. "We leave in five minutes. I'll eat as we drive," said Crowley.

While Crowley was finishing his cup of coffee, JD was busy cleaning up the BWC and getting their stuff ready to leave.

A few minutes later Crowley stood up and said, "Let's roll, boy." They then grabbed their stuff and headed out the door toward the Chevelle. Crowley popped the trunk, loaded their gear, then climbed into the driver's seat. Before firing up the engine, Crowley looked over at JD and said, "No matter what we find back at your home, you need to keep it together mentally until we complete our task, or we'll both die. I can't do this without you. I know that sounds cold, but it's a fact, and I don't have the luxury of sugarcoating anything."

"Don't worry, I understand. I'm mentally prepared for anything. I know what's at risk if we fail," replied JD.

"Good. You are becoming one tough little bastard," said Crowley with an admiring but short-lived grin.

Having said that, Crowley fired up the engine, and they sped off down the street, heading east toward Bangor, Maine.

What they saw as they traveled closer to Bangor left them in awe. Towns were completely empty, and there were abandoned cars all over the roads. There were no police, military, or any type of authorities to be seen. It was as if it was every man for himself. This didn't surprise either of them. No one could explain why people were mysteriously disappearing in droves at night, and no one, no matter what their job was, wanted to stick around to find out why. JD and Crowley also hadn't watched the news for quite some time, so they weren't sure what the government or authorities were even planning. They could only guess they were deciding to stay away until they could figure out what they were dealing with.

Several hours went by before they saw the sign that said they were entering Maine, and that meant they were only a few hours away from Bangor.

JD felt a sense of strangeness and uneasiness come over him as they crossed the state line into Maine. Crowley looked over at him, and JD knew he felt it as well.

Once JD saw the sign that said they were entering Bangor, a feeling of despair hit him, like someone had just kicked him in the gut. He tried his damndest to focus on the task at hand and what they needed to accomplish.

"We'll head straight to your home and park on the street with the car facing west, in case we need to leave in a hurry for whatever reason," said Crowley.

JD just nodded his head.

As they drove closer and closer to JD's home, they could see the town was completely deserted. Front doors to houses were wide open, and people's clothes and possessions littered the streets.

LXVI

As they pulled onto the street that JD lived on, Crowley slowed the Chevelle down to a slow crawl. All of his friends' houses were on the same street as JD's. His was at the end of the cul-de-sac. As they drove past each one of his friends' houses, JD could see the front doors were wide open. When they pulled up to JD's house, he immediately noticed the front door was open as well. He looked on in horror, as he could see there were red stains all over the front door, leading out onto the driveway, then the blood suddenly stopped at the edge of the cement.

Without thinking, JD jumped out of the Chevelle and raced for the front door. "Damn it, boy! Stop! We need to enter with caution," said Crowley as he also jumped out and quickly followed JD into the house.

When Crowley entered the front living room of JD's house, he immediately stopped in his tracks, right behind JD. The horror that had stopped JD from proceeding any farther was immediately obvious. The house was covered in blood, everywhere. It was as if someone had bathed the house in blood. JD fell to his knees in shock, unable to even cry.

Crowley didn't hesitate in saying, "This certainly wasn't the work of the Malum, boy. They don't leave this much trace when they consume someone. Blood is what they want, and they wouldn't waste so much of it. I'm not sure what the hell happened here, but I assume we'll find out."

Crowley's voice took a sterner tone with the next sentence. "JD, this is where you need to push through and be strong. We must reach Smith Cemetery before dark."

He put his hand on JD's shoulder, letting him know he understood that he was in pain. JD knew what needed to be done and immediately stood up, turned around, and walked toward the front door. He stopped halfway through the doorway and turned around, looking at Crowley. "Let's go kill this fucker!"

Cowley nodded his head in agreement and followed JD toward the Chevelle's trunk. Crowley popped the trunk, grabbed the chainsaw, a sawed-off shotgun he'd gotten from Harmonia, and a black backpack containing a rope, knife, flashlights, and other various supplies, in case they should need them. JD grabbed the red gas can, which had been refilled with gas, along with the silver .357 pistol. They both turned around without shutting the trunk and started walking toward the trail that would lead them to Smith Cemetery.

"You lead the way, boy. Keep your eyes and ears on alert. I know it's daytime, but something has been bothering me ever since we entered Maine. Something is off. I know you feel it as well."

"Got it," replied JD.

When they made it to the beginning of the mountain trail in JD's backyard, JD paused for a moment. Finally, he stepped onto the trail. A flood of memories of his friends and parents came racing into his mind. He was again hit with an immense amount of emotional pain and anguish, realizing he would most likely never see any of them again. As quickly as those emotions entered his mind, he forced them out and proceeded to step onto the mountain trail and started hiking toward the cemetery.

As they were hiking along, getting closer to the cemetery with each step, JD couldn't help but reminisce about his childhood and the good times he and his friends spent in these hills, running around raising hell. With everything that had happened, those memories were still able to bring a smile to his face.

After a few minutes of reminiscing, JD reminded himself of what lay ahead, and the smile was gone from his face as quickly as it had appeared.

After thirty minutes of hiking, JD suddenly stopped and said in a whisper, "We're not far from the cemetery now. I'd say another fifteen minutes."

"All right, boy, that's good, we're on schedule. We should have a few minutes to spare when we get there before the sun sets," replied Crowley.

LXVI

JD took a deep breath, mustered up some courage, and continued hiking toward the cemetery. As he was hiking, he continually looked over to the west, at the sun, to make sure they had plenty of light left. When the cemetery came into view, both Crowley and JD slowed their pace down substantially. For some reason unknown to them, they tried to be as quiet as possible as they hiked along, carefully picking their way along the trail. As they got closer and closer, a horrible sense of dread came over them. They both knew this feeling was very different than what they'd encountered at the Verwer farm. Something was definitely wrong.

"Be ready, boy. I know you're sensing it as well," said Crowley in a whisper.

Instead of replying, JD just nodded his head, showing he understood.

As they got closer and closer to the cemetery gates, the black pillar came into view. Flashbacks of the night it all started came flooding back into JD's mind, like someone was punching him in the head. JD could hear Matthew's blood-curdling screams as the Malum consumed him.

The hair on his arms stood on end.

They proceeded to walk into the cemetery and could see the torn and bloodied clothes of policemen and jackets that read Search and Rescue Team. There were even a few dog collars scattered throughout the cemetery from the scent dogs the men had brought. JD and Crowley didn't have to guess what had happened to them.

They both walked straight over to the black pillar, looked at each other, and Crowley gave JD the nod, meaning it was time to douse the black pillar in gasoline. JD opened the red can of gas and proceeded to douse the black pillar until every last drop was gone from the can. While JD was pouring gasoline on the pillar, Crowley was scanning the area, trying to figure out what felt so wrong and why they were sensing something different.

"Light up the pillar, boy, and let me know as soon as the sun sets behind the mountains. We're only a few minutes away now," said Crowley, as he fired up the chainsaw and gunned it, getting it warmed up, ready to chew through the black pillar.

JD lit a match and tossed it on the pillar, sending flames soaring into the air. As Crowley was gunning the chainsaw, JD heard what sounded like a gunshot ring out. He then saw Crowley hitting the ground along with the chainsaw, bringing the chainsaw to a screeching halt. JD quickly turned around to see where the shot had come from, and to his horrific and unimaginable surprise, he saw Matthew's parents come walking slowly out of the trees, each of them carrying a gun that was pointed directly at him.

"That's right, JD, don't stand there looking so surprised. Matthew had been trying for a very long time to get you boys into this cemetery, so we could unleash the Malum into this miserable world. Only thing is, he had no idea why he was wanting to do it," said Mac.

"You bastards! He was your son! Why?" shouted JD.

"A sacrifice had to be made in order for us to become complete Hexies, and now we're almost complete. Did you find the present we left for you at your house?" said Matthew's mother, Michelle, with a slight grin stretching her lips.

That last sentence hit JD right to the core. He knew in that instant he would never see his parents alive again. He then went into such a deep state of shock he could say nothing or do nothing but just stand there, ready to die. He was tired of fighting. He was ready to meet his friends and family again.

"Now it's time for you two to get consumed by the Malum. It won't be long now before the sun sets, and we'll become complete Hexies," said Mac, as he and Michelle kept their guns pointed at JD.

All the while they were talking, Crowley, who was still alive, had been slowly moving to grab the sawed-off shotgun that was just to his right. JD caught the movement out of the corner of his eye, and he looked down at Crowley, who was looking back up at him. Crowley winked at him, took aim, and fired a slug round from the shotgun, hitting Mac directly in the chest and leaving behind a hole the size of a softball. This sent Mac stumbling backwards over a gravestone, dying almost instantly. Michelle, who was still pointing her gun at JD, was caught off guard, but in her now panicked state, she suddenly pulled the trigger of her weapon, sending off a bullet that went ripping through the lower left side of JD's abdomen.

At first, all JD felt was a wet, warm, burning sensation on his left side. Then he was hitting the ground in excruciating pain as he faced Crowley. Right then, he saw Crowley fire off another round from the shotgun, this time at Michelle, hitting her in the face, which sent pieces of her face and skull flying everywhere. JD was reeling in pain as Crowley managed to stand up and snatch the chainsaw off the ground, lifting it into the air above his head as he gunned its engine. Crowley then let out a roar that was as loud as the chainsaw itself. He brought the chainsaw down to the bottom of the black pillar and gunned it even more as it started chewing through the black pillar. The horrific scream they'd both heard before at the Verwer farm came once again, as the thick, black liquid substance came squirting out of the black pillar, flying through the air as the chainsaw growled its way through the pillar.

One of the last things JD remembered before blacking out was Crowley standing over the cut-down black pillar trying to catch his breath, while clutching his right shoulder. The very last thing he remembered was Crowley collapsing to the ground.

I'm not sure how long either of us were out—might've been hours, might've been days. We were both awakened, though, by the warmth of the sun hitting our faces and the strong smell of blood in the air.

"Boy, you still alive?" asked Crowley as he struggled to sit up, clutching his right shoulder in pain.

"Yeah, but I feel like hell, like a dump truck ran over me. The bullet ripped through the left side of my belly, passing clean through. It must not've hit anything important, otherwise I don't think I'd be here now," replied JD.

"I'm getting too old for this shit," said Crowley, as he grabbed the closest gravestone with his left hand and pulled himself up into a standing position. "I'm still having a hard time grasping the fact that Matthew's parents were the cause of all of this, and that they'd sacrifice their own son. I've witnessed some fucked-up things during my existence on this planet, but this one comes close to the most horrific of them all. Undeniable proof that dark evil does exist in mankind," said Crowley.

JD, who was still lying on the ground, trying to gain his composure and gather enough strength to stand up, said, "Matthew also had two younger sisters. I'm worried about them. I'm not sure I want to find out what happened to them."

"If their parents didn't do something to them, then they must've escaped town, otherwise they would have used them as their remaining sacrifices to the Malum, and their transformations would've been complete," said Crowley.

Crowley then slowly walked over to JD and lowered his hand to help him stand up. They were both in extreme amounts of pain and both covered in blood. When JD finally stood up, they both stood there looking around for several minutes, neither one saying a word.

They then turned their attention to the bloodied bodies of Matthew's parents where they were lying on the ground.

"I hope those two bastards burn in hell," said JD.

"I have no doubt they are, boy," replied Crowley.

Crowley turned around, slowly bent over, and struggled in pain to pick up his backpack and the shotgun that had saved both of their lives. "Let's see if we can hike down out of here, boy."

"Got it," said JD as he reached down and picked up the silver .357 revolver.

They looked like they'd just gotten the shit kicked out of them as they slowly stumbled out of the cemetery and onto the trail that would lead them down the mountain.

LXVI

It was a surprisingly warm, sunny, beautiful day for late fall, which was usually cold in Bangor. As they slowly hiked down the trail, both of them took notice of the mountains around them and how beautiful they looked. They'd each gained a new perspective on life because they had both resigned themselves to the fact they were going to die.

As JD hiked along the trail, he especially tried to soak it all in because he knew there might be a chance he'd never see this area again. Now that his parents were both dead, as far as he knew anyway, there was no reason for him to stay here. Staying in this town would only cause him pain.

It took several long, painful hours of slowly walking and stumbling along before JD's house finally came into view. By now the sun was farther in the west, meaning it was late afternoon. They still had no idea how long they had been passed out in the cemetery, but it didn't matter because there was nowhere they needed to be.

When they made it to JD's backyard and stepped off the trail and onto the grass, Crowley looked at JD and said, "Go into your house and grab the stuff you want, boy. You'll be going with me back to Harmonia's. I'll wait out here."

JD just nodded his head and slowly walked into his house. He tried to avoid looking at the blood that covered the living room and kitchen as he made his way upstairs to his parents' and his bedrooms. He stopped first at his parents' bedroom and stood there looking at the bed they used to sleep in, which was neat and made up like always when they weren't sleeping in it. A wave of emotion hit him like a brick wall, and tears started streaming down his face. He thought back to the many nights when he was younger, when they'd sit on that bed and talk about his day after he'd come home from school or from playing outside with his friends.

After a few minutes JD turned around and went into his bedroom to gather some of his things. He immediately noticed a letter sitting on his bed with his name on it. He picked it up, opened it, and all it said was: *We love you, son. Mom and Dad.*

Even with tears streaming down his face, he was able to smile slightly and say aloud, "I love you too, Mom and Dad, wherever you are."

He picked up his big hockey bag and emptied out the contents. He wouldn't need his hockey stuff where he was headed. He then gathered some of his things, along with the letter, and put them into the hockey bag and walked out of the house. He saw Crowley sitting on the curb with his back to him.

Crowley looked back at him and asked, "Ready, boy?"

"Yeah, I'm ready, old man," replied JD.

"Good, 'cause you have to drive Black Beauty," said Crowley.

"Is that what you call her?" asked JD with a chuckle.

"Yes, but no one knows that except you, and let's keep it that way," replied Crowley with a smirk.

They both slowly walked over to the already-open trunk of the car and put their stuff in it. JD shut the trunk, since Crowley wasn't able to use his right arm. They then climbed in and sat down as both of them murmured in pain as their butts and backs hit the bucket seats of the Chevelle.

JD reached up and flipped the sun visor down, dropping the keys into his lap. He picked up the keys, inserted the ignition key, fired up Black Beauty, and gunned the engine, letting the horses roar.

Crowley looked over at JD and said, "Let's get the hell outta here, boy."

JD put the Chevelle into drive and sped off down that empty road, heading west.